MARRIAGE CAN BE MURDER

The victim, Al Greenberg, had a bad heart, but not an enemy in the world—except Samantha. Once she'd wanted to be in pictures. She'd landed nothing more than a humiliating role on the casting couch.

Had Samantha returned as Phoebe Greenberg, who never dropped a tear at her husband's demise but picked up five million bucks? Or as Lenore Tulley, married to the studio's biggest star, who told everyone to "drop dead" and meant every word? Or as Trude Burke, the PR man's wife, whose strawberry blond hair was as phony as her past?

Murder expert Masao Masuto was about to have a heart condition of his own to consider, when looking for the lethal lady led to unexpected love . . . and a murderer determined to give a repeat performance.

BY E. V. CUNNINGHAM

The Case of
the Angry Actress

E. V. CUNNINGHAM

A DELL BOOK

Published by
Dell Publishing Co., Inc.
1 Dag Hammarskjold Plaza
New York, New York 10017

This work was first published
under the title SAMANTHA.

Dell ® TM 681510, Dell Publishing Co., Inc.

ISBN: 0-440-11093-9

Reprinted by arrangement with the author
Printed in the United States of America
First Dell printing—June 1984
D D

To the memory of
Nat Goldstone
good friend

The Main Cast

STOCKHOLDERS IN NORTHEASTERN FILMS

Al Greenberg, who is married to Phoebe
Murphy Anderson, who is married to Stacy
Sidney Burke, who is married to Trude
Jack Cotter, who is married to Arlene
Mike Tulley, who is married to Lenore

POLICEMEN

Beverly Hills: Detective Sergeant Masao Masuto
                 (Kati, his wife)
                 Detective Sy Beckman
                 Officer Frank Seaton
                 Medical Examiner Dr. Sam Baxter

Los Angeles: Lieutenant Pete Bones
                Detective Kelly

And numerous others who appear in good time
and without confusion.

CHAPTER ONE

Al Greenberg

In Beverly Hills, as in so many of the cities, towns and villages of the United States, there is a right and a wrong side of the tracks. The tracks in this case belong to the Southern Pacific Railroad, and they bisect the town from west to east, departing, as they say, no more than a whoop and a holler from the Pacific Ocean. North of Santa Monica Boulevard—upon which the railroad runs—is possibly the most compact conglomeration of rich people that exists anywhere in the world. Southward, to Wilshire Boulevard, is a very posh little shopping area, and south from Wilshire Boulevard lies the "poor" section of Beverly Hills, where you can still buy a one-family house for forty-five thousand dollars.

Detective Sergeant Masao Masuto, of the Beverly Hills Police Force, did not live in the "poor" section of Beverly Hills. He lived in a cottage in Culver City and considered himself most fortunate to be possessed of the cottage, a good wife, three children, and a rose garden upon which he lavished both love and toil. He secretly dreamed of himself as a gardener who devoted all of his working hours to his garden.

He was driving home this evening and dreaming this particular and favorite dream, when the radiotelephone in the car flickered. He picked up the telephone and was informed by the sergeant in charge of dispatching that

evening that a man named Al Greenberg was dead in a
house on North Canon Drive, and that the circumstances
under which the death had occurred might be regarded as
somewhat suspicious.

Would he go directly there?

He would. He was on Pico Boulevard, and now he
swung into Beverly Drive—a matter of minutes from the
address on North Canon Drive.

Detective Masuto knew the address, the place, the house,
just as he knew almost every address, place and house in
Beverly Hills. This was not as much of an achievement as
it sounds. Where he entered Beverly Hills from the south,
driving from Pico across Olympic and then up to Wilshire,
the city was only thirty-five blocks wide, and that was
about its greatest width, even though it extended a long
finger into the foothills of the Santa Monica range. North
of Santa Monica Boulevard there were the great elegant
streets with their palms, their perfect lawns and their quarter-
of-a-million-dollar houses, and these streets Detective Masuto
could visualize and name, from Trenton Drive on the west,
to Walden, Linden, Roxbury, Bedford, Camden, Rodeo,
Beverly and Canon—and after Canon, moving east,
Crescent, Rexford, Alpine, Foothill, Elm, Maple, Palm,
Hillcrest, Arden, Alta, Sierra and Oakhurst—and there the
city within a city ended and became Los Angeles. In Los
Angeles, there were people and poverty and poolrooms
and whorehouses and high-rise apartments and various
other ordinary, publicly owned urban equipment. In Beverly Hills, there were property, money and some people.

As his chief of police had explained it to him once,
"This is like no other place in the world, Masao. The
money is God; the property is sacred; and the people are to
be handled with kid gloves until you know who they
are—and mostly they are the kind of people you handle
with kid gloves after you know who they are."

"Kid gloves." He was a California-born Japanese, and

therefore he was an Oriental and not a white man by any means, but excellent with kid gloves.

"The hell with that," he said to himself now. "You have a job, my boy—not a bad job."

He knew the house on North Canon, and he knew who lived there and when they had moved in and how much they had paid for the house and what it was worth today, three years later. Naturally. He knew every house. He knew that "Canon" without accent or similar indication was pronounced "Cannon" by some natives—if you can speak of dwellers in Beverly Hills as natives—and "Canyon" by others. He used the latter pronounciation, as had Al Greenberg, who now lay dead in the house on North Canon. He remembered a small conversation he had with Greenberg concerning the word "Canon." Greenberg, very rich, had also been very curious, and Masuto could not help liking curious people—he was so hopelessly curious himself.

Now Greenberg was dead, a short, stout wistful man of sixty-two or three, in a great antebellum type of house with outside pillars two stories high, a proper part of a *Gone With the Wind* sound stage dropped between a Spanish Colonial and an eighteen-room Irish cottage. Greenberg had never been greatly at ease in that house, as Masuto remembered. He had sensitivity, and there was always a shred of shame hanging out of his pocket as if he had never answered the question as to what a small Jew, born and brought up in Bensonhurst in Brooklyn, was doing here in this garden of dreams, repose and dolce vita. It was certainly not de rigueur to be seen on your front lawn at any hour of the day if you lived in Beverly Hills and north of Santa Monica, but Detective Masuto could remember many a late afternoon when he saw Al Greenberg standing in front of the misplaced plantation house, puffing a cigar and regarding the green palm and ivy world that surrounded him with wonder and disbelief.

No more wonder and no more disbelief. Al Greenberg was dead, and they had called the cops.

Masuto double-parked in front of the huge Southern-Colonial plantation house on North Canon. In the drive-way of the house were three cars, and five more were parked in front and two more already double-parked; among them, as Masuto noticed, two police cars and two medical cars, one of them belonging to Dr. Sam Baxter, the medical examiner. When Masuto got out of his car, he was met by Detective Sy Beckman, who informed him that Officer Frank Seaton was inside the house and another officer stationed at the door.

"What was it? What went on here tonight?"

"Dinner party—black tie, old buddies, but very formal. Four couples and the host and wife. That's Al Greenberg. He's dead."

"I know. I got that in the car. How was he killed?"

"He wasn't killed. Maybe. He died."

"Of what?" Masuto asked as he and Beckman walked up the path to the house. The planting was old and good, and the air was full of the sweet smell of jasmine. Masuto was never unaware of a planting, and he tasted the cool evening air, mingling his pleasure at the smell with his forlorn reaction to death.

"A heart attack. Baxter's inside and so is Dr. Meyer, Greenberg's physician. I think you better talk to both of them."

"Oh?"

"I mean before you talk to the others."

"All there?"

"They want out, but I'm holding them for you. Nothing has leaked yet, unless some smart reporter was listening on the radio band. There was nobody up at headquarters, and the boss is of the opinion that we should keep it absolutely quiet until we know something."

"What?"

"That it's murder or not murder."

"You said he died of a heart attack."

"That's what the doctors say. One of the guests says different."

"Who?"

Detective Beckman peered at his pad in the poor light that seeped from the windows onto the veranda.

"Feller named Jack Cotter."

Masuto nodded, and then the door was opened by a young and very pretty strawberry blonde, who silently and with a funereal air ushered them into the house. Officer Seaton, a tall uniformed patrolman, came up then and apologized for his partner, who was using the bathroom at the back of the house.

"The doctors are in the living room there," he said, pointing over his shoulder. "The rest of them are in the viewing room."

The viewing room was par for this particular course, Masuto reflected, hardly listening to the blonde's explanation that this was where "poor Al" showed films. He was looking at the stately double staircase and spread of the living room beyond, and without even glancing at the blonde, he asked her name.

"Trude Burke—Mrs. Sidney Burke."

"Then would you join the others in the viewing room, Mrs. Burke, and tell them that I would like to talk to them in a few minutes."

"You're very official, aren't you, Detective—?"

"Masuto."

"I thought you were Japanese. Good-looking. You know—"

"Please do as I say, Mrs. Burke."

"I just thought I'd be here to greet the big brass and let them know that there's no murder, and it is all a lot of nonsense, and suppose we all go home and leave poor Phoebe with her grief, such as it is."

"Please do as I say, and later you can tell me all about that."

The other officer came back to the front door. Masuto regarded him without pleasure, waited for Trude Burke to disappear, and then followed Beckman into the living room, where two middle-aged physicians were restlessly observing their wrist watches. Dr. Baxter, the medical examiner—tall, skinny, gray, and tired—shook hands with Masuto and introduced him to Dr. Meyer. Masuto had heard about Meyer, successful, reputable, and expensive.

"What happened?"

"Tell him," Dr. Baxter said impatiently. "The facts, not the nonsense. Beckman can feed him the nonsense after you and I go about our business."

"Mr. Greenberg was a patient of mine," Dr. Meyer said. "He has suffered for many years from angina. Quite bad. Tonight he had an attack and he died. Very quickly."

"What kind of an attack?" Masuto asked him.

"A heart attack, of course. Coronary. There was a myocardial infarction, and he passed away."

"Quickly?"

"Yes. Before he could reach his medicine."

Masuto turned to Baxter. "Do you agree, doctor?"

"Absolutely."

"No other possibility?"

"There is none that I can see, officer," Meyer said. "No other is being offered. Jack Cotter, who is here and who is Mr. Greenberg's business associate, has made a very serious accusation—namely that Mr. Greenberg was threatened and frightened to death. He calls it murder. I have no desire to comment on the legal aspect or even on the social aspect concerning what happened in this house. I came here. My friend and patient was dead. I examined him and did what I could—which was nothing. This is not a house I enjoy being in at this moment, and there is no grief here for me to assuage. So I wish to go."

"Could Mr. Greenberg have died of fright? Or excitement?" Masuto asked.

"Of course. That's the nature of the disease. Or of ten other trigger causes."

"Is there no way to tell?"

"None."

"Even with an autopsy?"

"No way."

"And you agree?" Masuto asked the medical examiner.

"Yes, Masao. Absolutely."

"Just one or two more questions, Dr. Meyer, and then you can leave. Did you expect Mr. Greenberg to die so suddenly?"

"How does one know?"

"But you must have had some idea of how bad the disease was."

"Of course I had some idea. I had a very good picture of his sickness."

"Suppose he was a lucky man—which he was not. How long might he have lived?"

"Ten years—twelve. You simply cannot pinpoint it. Maybe five years—maybe twice that. Would you like to see his body?"

Masuto nodded, and Meyer led him upstairs to the master bedroom, where under a sheet the mortal remains of Al Greenberg reposed. Masuto uncovered Greenberg's face and looked at him for a long moment.

The living room was French, a combination of several Louis', with a huge, pale Aubusson carpet. The viewing room was practical leather—two enormous leather couches and half a dozen leather lounge chairs. At one end, the projection room, at the other the screen—but both now concealed behind beige drapes. A third wall, where the drapes were drawn back, revealed the planting behind the house, a small tropical jungle which separated the house from the swimming pool. A well-equipped bar and an orange rug completed the furnishings.

There were nine people sprawled on the couches and chairs, and they all looked at the door with a more or less common expression of sullen annoyance as the two men entered, Detective Beckman with Masuto behind him. Death muted them, yet they were annoyed and put upon. One of them, a lean, good-looking man in his middle forties, said something about house arrest being a little less than to his liking. "I have had about enough of it," he said tartly.

There were four men and five women in the room. Masuto recognized the man who had spoken. His name was Mike Tulley, for years a small part player in Westerns, who now was a sort of star in television terms. He had a program of his own called "Lonesome Rider," and his rating was high and he earned well over three thousand dollars a week.

Another man, older, tall, with white wavy hair and very certain of his presence, rose and came toward the detectives. "Easy does it," he said. "We're all under a strain, you know. My name is Murphy Anderson. I was Al's—that is, Mr. Greenberg's lawyer. Also his business associate. We've all been shaken by his death—" He had addressed his words to Masuto.

"You are a policeman, aren't you?" he added.

"That's right."

"You're in charge here?"

"With my colleague, Detective Beckman."

Masuto absorbed the room. You listened and absorbed; you were conscious of many things, which was in the manner of his life and way, and you pressed conclusions away from you. He noted the five women in the room. There was the strawberry blonde, whom he had seen at the door. There was a girl with dark hair. The other three were blondes. But all five, in the particular manner of Beverly Hills, could have been cast from the same mould. Two of them rose after he entered and then slipped onto the chair arms. Another went to the bar and mixed a drink. All appeared to be about the same height, each with the same trim, tight figure. Even their faces were alike, noses tip-tilted, mouths full. They were a part of a social organism that demanded beauty and alikeness, yet each was different, separate, unique. One of them he recognized—Phoebe Greenberg, widow of the dead man. She was neither pros-trated nor weeping, but since she could hardly be more than thirty, with a husband who had been sixty-three and ill and very rich, this was not a matter for surprise.

Of the men, he had recognized only the actor, Mike Tulley. Now he added Murphy Anderson, lawyer, to the file. Anderson would be about fifty. He introduced the widow, then his own wife, Mrs. Anderson, the girl with the dark hair. Then Murphy Anderson introduced Trude Burke, the strawberry blonde.

"I am Detective Sergeant Masuto, Beverly Hills police," Masao Masuto said politely. "I understand that this is a strain for everyone concerned."

The youngest man in the room rose and introduced himself as Sidney Burke, the head of a successful PR agency. That made him the husband of the strawberry blonde. He was about thirty-seven, small, tight, competent, with pebble-black eyes. Tough, dangerous, wily—all words that Masuto remembered and discarded. You simply did not know. It took time.

"More than that, it's a stupid imposition," Burke said.

Masuto's eyes deliberately avoided the final couple. The remaining man, fleshy, balding but once quite handsome, with a long, thin nose and excellent chin and mouth, pinged on the detective's memory. He had been a sort of a star—just after World War II—but briefly. Then a very successful agent—or was it a producer?

He rose and said, "My name is Jack Cotter, officer. This is my wife, Arlene—"

Of course, the agent. And now Al Greenberg's vice-president in Northeastern Films.

"—and I am afraid that I am responsible for the imposition. Entirely responsible. You see, I have made a damn nuisance of myself by insisting that Al was murdered."

"You can say that again!" Tulley snorted.

"A veritable goddamn nuisance," said Burke.

"Suppose you shut up, Sidney. You talk when you're told to talk," Tulley, the TV actor, said.

"Just who the hell do you think you're putting down?" Burke demanded. "I don't work for you, mister. You're a client of mine, and now that Al's dead, I don't want such clients. So up your ass!"

"Take it easy, Sidney," Murphy Anderson said. "You too, Mike," he told the actor. "Just take it easy. Jack heard something, and not to report what he heard would make him an accessory after the fact."

"What fact?" Sidney Burke demanded.

"The fact of a murder—if a murder took place. I don't like the whole thing any more than any of you, but there it is—"

Masuto held up his hands for silence at this point. Being a policeman in Beverly Hills might not be exactly like being a diplomat to the Benelux countries. It might be better compared to being a UN representative to a small, new country. It required tact, judgement, and above all, good manners—and control.

"Ladies and gentlemen," he said, "the sooner and the more quietly we conclude this, the better. As you know, Mr. Greenberg was quite ill, and it would appear that he died of natural causes. But appearances are frequently deceiving. Now if you heard something, Mr. Cotter, that bears on Mr. Greenberg's death, I think you should state it for me in as few words as possible, while we are all still here."

Cotter nodded. "We finished dinner a few minutes after nine. Ordinarily, we might sit at the table awhile, but Al did not feel too good, and he said that he'd go upstairs and have an Alka Seltzer. Everyone got up. Then the girls left with Mike and Sidney and Al. I am told that Al went up to his bedroom on the second floor. The kitchen people said that. Al went through the kitchen to the pantry, where he has a little private elevator. The others went into the living room.''

''Sidney and I went into the viewing room—here,'' Mike Tulley interrupted. ''The girls went to freshen up.''

''All right,'' said Cotter. ''Murph—Mr. Anderson—and I sat at the table with cigars. We had things to talk about, and then Murph said about something that before we discussed it any further, we should get Al's point of view. It was almost a yes or no matter, so Murph said that he would wait at the table while I went upstairs. I went through the living room and up the stairs. No one in the hallway up there. I knocked at Al's bedroom door. Then I heard Al say, 'For Christ's sake, put that gun away and give me my medicine—please—' He was pleading, crazy, desperate, pleading. He was pleading for his life.''

Out of the corner of his eye, Masuto saw Dr. Baxter, the medical examiner, come into the viewing room, and he moved his head for Baxter to join him. Cotter waited. The room was very quiet now. Baxter walked over to Masuto, who whispered to him, ''Medicine?''

''He was on quinidine according to Meyer, but also armed with nitroglycerin sublingual. He would have that in his pocket. Every angina does. But his jacket was off and across the room from where he lay.''

Baxter spoke softly, but not so softly that everyone in the room could not hear him. Phoebe Greenberg began to cry. She must have washed off her makeup and she was pretty without it. It occurred to Masuto that perhaps she had wept earlier. Emotion and the display of emotion by the population of Beverly Hills was not anything that Masuto felt competent to analyze or predict.

''Please continue,'' he said to Cotter.

''Yes—of course,'' Cotter said. ''Al was pleading, and then this dame's voice says, 'Like you gave me mine, you bastard—remember?' And Al pleads again, 'Please, please—' Then I start banging on the door and I hear a thud. I hear Al fall, I guess, but the door is locked. I know that Al's room and Phoebe's are connected. Each of them has a dressing room that leads into a bathroom, and the two bathrooms connect. So I run to Phoebe's room—I guess I did some shouting. In Phoebe's room, I saw Stacy—Murph's wife—she was lying on the bed, resting. Then I bust through the connecting rooms to Al's room, and there's Al on the floor, dead. I didn't know he was dead then, but that's what Meyer said. So I go to unlock the hall door and get help, but it's already unlocked. And that's it.''

Still silence. Most of them were watching Cotter, not the detective, who said, "Whose voice did you hear, Mr. Cotter?''

"Don't you think we asked him that?'' Sidney Burke said. "The other cop asked him. But he's playing cute. Real cute. Now he's going to take you into the next room and pin it on his choice.''

"Oh, why don't you shut up,'' Cotter said tiredly. "What I got to say, I say right here. Murph's my lawyer, and he's here. I don't know whose voice it was. Whoever the dame was, she was crazy mad. Her voice was choking and hoarse. I don't know whose voice it was.''

"But it was a woman's voice—of that you're certain?''

"I never gave it a second thought.''

"A man's voice can sound like a woman's voice.''

"No.''

"Very well,'' Masuto said, smiling sympathetically. "Dr. Baxter here—'' pointing to him, "—is our local medical examiner. It is his opinion at this moment that no crime has been committed, that Mr. Greenberg died of natural causes—''

"How in hell you can talk like that after what I heard, I don't know!'' Cotter burst out.

"Please, Mr. Cotter—what you heard indicates that violence might have threatened Mr. Greenberg. It would appear, from what you tell me, that a woman was in the room with Mr. Greenberg and that she threatened him with a gun. But it would also appear that Mr. Greenberg's heart attack had already started. Possibly this woman or person refused to hand Mr. Greenberg the sublingual tablets upon which his life depended. We don't know, and we also do not know that a crime has been committed. Murder is a very ugly matter, Mr. Cotter, and for the moment I feel it would be best for everyone concerned to refrain from using the word. This does not mean that we will not pursue our investigation. We certainly shall. But for tonight—well, I think Mr. Anderson will agree with me."

"I certainly do!" Anderson said emphatically.

"Then I think that if I may ask a few questions, brief and to the point, you can then leave. No more than ten minutes."

"I think I have had about all I can stand," Phoebe Greenberg said softly.

"Then two questions and you can leave. Firstly, do you own a gun or is there a gun anywhere in this house?"

"No."

"And where were you when Mr. Cotter shouted?"

"Apparently I was in the pantry elevator on my way up to the second floor. When I got out, there was the commotion—and Al was dead."

"I felt bad," Stacy Anderson said. "That's why I went up to Phoebe's room to lie down. Phoebe said she would bring me a cup of tea. But Al was in his room already, and the doors were closed—two doors, so I could not hear anything. Not possibly."

"Then you went into the kitchen?" Masuto asked Phoebe.

"The pantry. We have a hot-cold water cooler there. No one saw me, if that is what you mean."

"Thank you," Masuto said, bowing almost impercept- ably, a tribute to the lady of a house where he once had a friend, for even the small warmth of slight acquaintance is a form of friendship. "You may leave us now, and we will trouble your house only a few minutes more."

"Stay as long as you need to, please."

Masuto decided that he liked her. She either mourned the dead in her own way or not at all; it was her affair. He nodded to Baxter's unspoken question, and the doctor said, "I would like to have an autopsy done, Mrs. Greenberg."

"If you wish. If it will help."

"I think it will only help to put away doubts—but that's important."

"Then do as you see best."

And with that, she left the room.

Detective Masuto turned to Trude Burke.

"I was in the john," the strawberry blonde smiled. "I guess supper agreed with none of us."

"Where?"

"Front hall. Came out, heard the commotion, hotfooted it upstairs and almost fell over Arlene."

"You mean Mrs. Cotter?"

"Yes. Jack, her husband, was in the hall then, yelling for a doctor."

"Mrs. Cotter?"

Arlene Cotter rose, glanced quizzically at her husband and then nodded at Masuto. "No alibis—poor Oriental detective. I did not know there was a Nisei on our darling little police force. I was in the guest powder room, upstairs, when I heard the commotion and bounded into the hall. I went in there with Lenore Tulley—didn't I, darling?"

Lenore Tulley stared narrowly without replying. No love between them, Masuto decided. They were too alike: Beverly Hills twins, same height, same figure, same hairdresser.

"But then Lenore disappeared somewhere. Where did you disappear to, darling?"

"The pot, you bitch. You saw me go in there."

"Temper, temper," Arlene Cotter said.

"Then I went into the guest room, which connected with the guest bathroom," Lenore Tulley told Masuto. "To tell the truth, I was prowling. I have never been to this particular castle before. I was curious. Then I heard the commotion and stepped out into the hallway and joined the crowd in Al's bedroom."

Arlene Cotter smiled tolerantly. Mike Tulley watched them both intently, his wife and Cotter's wife.

"You remained at the dining room table?" Masuto asked Murphy Anderson.

"My cigar and I. I heard the commotion and then Sidney joined me. There is a small, spiral staircase in the projection booth, there—" he pointed, "—and first we thought something had happened in the viewing room. But it was empty. We went upstairs by the projection room staircase, which lets one into the far end of the upstairs hall."

"And before that, Mr. Burke?"

"I was with Mike Tulley in the viewing room. We were going to watch some shorts, and Mike was going to run them. He went into the projection booth. I mixed myself a drink and went into the dining room to see what had happened to the girls."

"Mr. Tulley?" Masuto said.

"Like Sidney says, I was in the projection booth, setting up the film. I heard the yelling from upstairs and I went up the staircase."

Beckman had been making notes. Now Masuto said, "I don't think we need trouble you further now. I would appreciate it if you would give pertinent facts, name, place, telephone to Detective Beckman here. Then you can leave. I think it would be wise if you say nothing about what Mr. Cotter heard—for the time being, that is."

"In other words, you are closing this up," Cotter said.

"No, Mr. Cotter, I am closing nothing. You can give your story to the press if you wish. I only feel that it might be better for everyone concerned if we waited a bit."

*   *   *

Detective Beckman was copying out his notes for Masuto, and Dr. Baxter was sipping at a glass of his dead host's excellent brandy, which the Japanese butler had poured for him. The house was staffed by a Japanese couple, not Niseis but recently come from Japan. The guests had departed. Mrs. Greenberg was asleep under the influence of a sedative; the guests had departed; and Al Greenberg's body had been taken to the hospital for the autopsy. The Japanese houseman was dutifully waiting for the policemen to depart, and Masao Masuto was explaining to his wife why he would be late. He spoke in Japanese quite deliberately. He wanted the houseman to overhear him, and when he had finished with the phone, he turned to the butler and said in Japanese, "What do you and your wife think of this?"

"Honorable official, we have no thoughts on the matter."

"That is nonsense, countryman of my father, as you well know. It is too late for witless formalities. I am not going to entrap you or arrest you, and not for a moment do I believe that you had anything to do with this. Do you think Mr. Greenberg was murdered?"

"No one hates such a man," the butler answered simply.

"All murders do not signify hate. What of the wife? Did they love each other?"

"They approached each other with respect. He was more than old enough to be her father."

"Would she kill him?"

"No."

"You are very sure."

"I am a man of small purpose—a house servant. I am poor and I must take what work is offered to earn my bowl of food. But I am not a fool."

"And where were you and your wife when this happened?"

"In the kitchen—where she is now. Would you speak with her?"

"No, it is not necessary. Go to her. I will call you when we are ready to leave."

The butler departed for the kitchen, and Baxter, the medical examiner, asked what it was all about.

"I asked him whether Phoebe Greenberg would have scalped her husband. He says no. He's a student of human nature, so I believe him. I don't have your Occidental gift for telling Jews from Gentiles. But Phoebe is not a Jewish name, is it?"

"Anything's a Jewish name today," Beckman said. "All the rules are broken. I'm a Jewish cop. But if you want to know about the girls—none of them is Jewish."

"How do you know?"

"I know. Take my word for it. About the men, I don't know with any confidence. I would guess that Greenberg was the only Jew in the lot. Maybe Murphy Anderson—"

"With a name like that!" Baxter snorted.

"I told you, names don't figure. It's all mixed up. By the way, Masao, this Mike Tulley, he whispers to me that you should give him half an hour to get home and then call him. I got his number here." He handed the number to Masuto, who nodded and said to Baxter, "What do you think, Doc?"

"I don't think. The autopsy will show absolutely nothing. Nothing. Greenberg died of a heart attack."

"Could fear have caused it?"

"Are you going to prove that, Masao? Come off it. If this is a murder, it's a perfect murder. File and forget. Even if one of those babes confesses to being in that bedroom and pointing a gun at Greenberg and refusing to get him the sublinguals, and you put me on the stand and read me the confession ten times over, I will still say that there is no evidence of murder or even reasonable doubt that the heart attack came from natural and inevitable causes. And I think any physician you get will agree with me. So if you got a murder, you got a perfect murder."

"A very few people on this earth," Masuto said

thoughtfully, "perfect themselves in all of their being and actions. Such people do not murder."

Then he dialed Mike Tulley's number.

Tulley answered and waited. Masuto reminded the TV actor that he had asked him to call, and then Tulley said, "I think we had better talk, Detective Masuto."

"It's past midnight. Can't it wait for tomorrow?"

"Maybe you sleep good. I take pills but that won't help tonight. I agree with Cotter. Greenberg was murdered."

"You're out in Benedict Canyon?"

"That's right. Five minutes from where you are."

"I'll be there," Masuto said. "Ten or fifteen minutes." He put down the phone and turned to Beckman. "He thinks Greenberg was murdered and he's frightened."

"Oh, balls," said the doctor. "I am going home to bed if you don't mind."

"Want me to come along with you, Masao?" Detective Beckman asked.

"No—no, you knock off, Sy. I'll see what he has to say. By the way, it seems to me that Anderson and Cotter were Greenberg's partners. Is that right?"

"I think so. Greenberg was the president of an outfit called Northeastern Films."

"And if I remember, I read somewhere that they produced the 'Lonesome Rider' or whatever that thing Tulley plays in is called."

"That's right—very big, successful. Number two on the Neilsen for seven months now. I read the *Hollywood Reporter*," Beckman explained to Dr. Baxter. "It's a sort of a damn trade journal, when you labor in Beverly Hills. I know where all the stars live. So does Masao. It gives us some kind of status among cops, but the pay remains lousy. Sidney Burke is press agent for Northeastern, according to what I heard tonight."

"Good night," Dr. Baxter said sourly.

Masuto called the Japanese houseman, said his good-bys

formally, and then he and Detective Baxter left. Officer Seaton was still outside, but Masuto felt it would be better to call no attention to the house, and he sent Seaton back to duty.

CHAPTER TWO

Mike Tulley

Mike Tulley's home was in Benedict Canyon just north of Lexington, or something over half a mile north of Sunset Boulevard. Three months before, the tourist sightseeing buses had taken to making a right turn on Sunset along Benedict—which was a tribute to his rating. The house was one hundred and fifty thousand dollars modern with a bean-shaped swimming pool and a carport wide enough to hold five cars.

Tulley was standing in the carport when Masuto drove up, and he was visibly relieved. He led Masuto toward the house, through the entranceway and living room to the library. Statuswise, this had replaced the den. There was a whole wall of fine leather bindings, Heritage Club, Limited Editions Club, and also several shelves of plain, common books purchased at Martindale's and at Mary Hunter's Bookshop. It made a good wall; people like Mike Tulley had little time for reading. There was an enormous antique globe and four Eames chairs. The couch, upholstered in black vinyl, was built in along one wall.

Tulley motioned for Masuto to sit down and asked whether he would have a drink. Masuto shook his head. Coffee? Again Masuto shook his head, and at that point Lenore Tulley stepped into the library and said, "You don't offer an Oriental coffee. Give him some tea."

"Lenore, suppose you go to bed. What I got to say to the detective here is private."

"You mean it stinks."

"You've had too much."

"Drop dead," she said, and swung around and left. Tulley stared hopelessly at Masuto.

Masuto waited. He was tired and unhappy, but he attempted to be patient and objective, without judgement or identification.

"Great! Great!" Tulley said. He poured himself a drink. "It's a great, stinking life. I am going to tell you something quick—because if I don't tell it quick, I can't tell it." He went to the door, opened it and then closed it again. "I wouldn't put it past her to have this place bugged," he said.

"Why don't you simply tell me whatever you wish to tell me."

"All right. Now look—this happened eleven years ago. I had a rotten small part in a TV thing they were doing at World Wide. They brought in some idiot kid who wanted a part—you got to know how these kids want a part. There are maybe ten thousand girls in this town who came here to make it big, and none of them do and they would sell their souls and their mothers for one stinking little part. So this kid is promised a part if she lets herself get banged once or twice—"

"Just spell that out, please," Masuto said.

"This guy makes a deal with her. He brings her into one of those little movable dressing rooms. She promises to have some sex with a couple of buddies. Then he invites me to be his guest. So I am a louse—you know a man who isn't a louse?"

"Go on, please."

"So I go in with this kid. I don't know how many there are before me. All I know is that I am invited to take a free ride, and I do it. In a crumby little dressing room with some kid I can barely see—except that she's a blond with a good figure. And she tells me her name and I kid her about the part and I hate myself a little and that's it."

Again, Masuto waited. Tulley was sprawled in the Eames chair. Masuto sat on the edge of the built-in couch. He was never at ease sprawling or reclining, and now he sat rather primly.

"I even forgot about it," Tulley said. "It was eleven years ago. Who remembers?"

"There are people who remember," Masuto said.

Tulley glanced at him sharply. Then he reached into his pocket, took out a card case and from it a folded piece of pink note paper. He unfolded it and handed it to the policeman. It was strongly scented and typed on it were the following words:

Mike, you've had your time and I have been patient.
                    Samantha.

Masuto handed it back to him. "I suppose Samantha was the girl?"

"That was her name. Would you believe it, I forgot. But when I got the note, I remembered."

"When did you get it?"

"In the mail, yesterday. I also know what typewriter was used."

"You do?"

He pointed to the wall opposite the couch, where a portable typewriter sat on a built-in teakwood table. "That one. I compared the type. There's a convenient broken 't' to make it easy. Do you want to keep this note?"

"If you wish." Masuto took the note and put it in his pocket. "Do you think your wife wrote it?"

"You saw her. She's not stupid, is she? Wouldn't she pick another typewriter?"

"I don't know. That is why I asked you."

Tulley stared at Masuto for a while, and then he said, "Something like this happens and you begin to think twice. I mean, nobody's stupid enough to do it this way, but she's smart enough to know we wouldn't believe she was stupid enough.''

''Why?'' Masuto asked softly. ''Do you think your wife is Samantha?''

He sat without answering.

''Eleven years ago, how old was this kid? Samantha?''

''Eighteen, nineteen, twenty—how the hell do you know?''

''You just told me it was eleven years ago. When did you meet your wife?''

''Six years ago.''

''An actress?''

Tulley nodded.

''When you go to bed with a woman, don't you look at her?'' Masuto asked coldly.

''I told you it was dark in that mousy dressing room.''

''Was Al Greenberg involved?''

''I think he was. I can't be sure, but I think I remember him on the set that day.''

''Cotter? Murphy Anderson? Sidney Burke?''

''I think so. Burke brought the girl onto the set.''

''How old is your wife, Mr. Tulley?''

''Thirty-one.''

''Do you think that your wife was in the room with Mr. Greenberg?''

''I don't know.''

''Do you own a gun?''

''We have a small thirty-two automatic. I keep it in the bedroom.''

''Obviously, you looked for it when you came home tonight. Was it there?''

''No.''

''And you asked your wife whether she knew where it was?''

''She didn't know. She said she couldn't care less. She hates guns and she has been after me to get rid of it.''

"Why don't you, Mr. Tulley? We have an excellent police force here in Beverly Hills."

"Which couldn't do one cotton-picking thing about keeping Al Greenberg alive."

"We are policemen, not physicians. Those men and women you had dinner with tonight—they have all been here at your home?"

"They have."

"Within the past two weeks?"

"That's right. We entertain a lot—dinner parties, cocktails. Sometimes when Al wanted a conference about the show, we would have it here."

"I see. But to get back to what you were inferring—is it your notion that this Samantha waited patiently for eleven years to have her revenge, and that she began by murdering Al Greenberg?"

"It sounds stupid when you put it that way. Maybe she waited for the one opportunity. Maybe she's patient. It still seems stupid."

"Farfetched, let's say. Still, someone wrote a note on your wife's typewriter and signed it 'Samantha.' "

"Don't you want to compare the note with a sample from the typewriter?"

"What will that prove, Mr. Tulley? If Samantha is patient enough to wait eleven years for her revenge, she's patient enough to wait for a chance at your wife's typewriter."

"What am I supposed to do?"

"I can't say, Mr. Tulley. If you believe you are in danger, you can inform my chief and he will no doubt station a policeman in front of your house."

"Just one thing," said Tulley, shooting out a hand at Masuto. "You're a cop—and this is Beverly Hills. So don't throw your weight around with me."

"I am very sorry if I gave that impression," Masuto said, smiling deferentially. "Thank you for your information."

Tulley's apology was contained in the gesture of rising and escorting Masuto to the door.

Masuto's wife was awake and waiting for him when he got home. She was very gentle and full of many fears, and when a case kept him hours past his regular working time, she could not sleep, and hovered over her two children and allowed her mind to fill with awful possibilities. Although she had been born in Los Angeles, her first years had been spent in an old-fashioned and protected environment, and she had many of the mannerisms of a girl brought up in Japan. Without trying, and very tastefully, she had given a Japanese decor to their little house in Culver City. She liked paper screens and low, black enamel tables, and both she and her husband, when they were alone for the evening, would wear kimono and robe; and tonight she had his robe waiting and tea ready, and she sat dutifully staring at him with great affection and waiting to hear whether he proposed to speak of what had happened.

"Al Greenberg died," he said finally, after he had tasted the tea and relaxed somewhat. "You will remember that when we ride with the children in Beverly Hills and I point out houses, his is the house with the great columns, like the big house in front of the old Selznick Studio."

"I am sorry to hear that. He was your friend."

"I think so. As much as anyone is a cop's friend."

"But why did they need the police?"

"One of the guests said that Mr. Greenberg was murdered."

"Was he?" she asked anxiously.

"I don't know. In the guise of being a philosophical Oriental type—which I am not—I would say that these people murder endlessly. Then there could be no death among them without the charge of murder being justified."

"I don't understand you."

"I am not sure that I want you to. Let's go to bed, and

perhaps I will stop dreaming, because this is like a nasty and turgid dream, pointless and with neither dignity nor honor.''

"Has it ever occured to you," Rabbi Matthew Gitlen asked Masuto the following morning, "to ponder on the curious parable of the camel and the needle's eye, and the rich man and the gates of heaven? A member of my congregation once coined a rather famous line to the effect that he had been rich and he had been poor and rich was better. The poor are too often maligned when they are accused of happiness, and the rich are maligned by the same accusation. As incredible as it may seem, I preach occasionally to my congregation—in my own words of course—that the Kingdom of God is within them. Which can be a dilly, you know. Are you a Christian? I ask in the most perfunctory professional sense, not to pry—simply to find a manner of discussing your inquiry. I trust the question does not embarrass you?''

"Not at all," Masuto replied, smiling. The rabbi was an enormous man, almost six-foot-four, Masuto would guess, very fat and apparently very civilized, but big enough in his frame to wear his weight with great dignity and to give the impression that a very large and hard-muscled man carried around another, a fat man, not out of indulgence but out of compassion. It had a curious effect on Masuto, who was put at his ease and who continued, "But I am not a Christian. I was never baptized. I am a Zen Buddhist— but that is not to be thought of as a religion in your sense.''

"I reject the obvious comment, and I am utterly fascinated," the rabbi rumbled, rising from behind his desk and going to one corner of his study, where there was a small refrigerator with a wood finish. He opened it and peered inside. "Will you join me in a yogurt, Detective Masuto? Supposedly, it reduces me, which is nonsense. A Zen Buddhist.''

"It would be my pleasure," Masuto said.

"Plain or orange or strawberry?"

"Plain, if I may."

"Of course." He handed Masuto a cup of yogurt and a spoon and sat on a corner of his desk as he opened his own. "Zen," he said. "What do they say? 'Those who know, speak not. Those who speak, know not.' Do you subscribe to that?"

"Oh, no—not at all," Masuto answered. "Everything can be spoken of, poorly perhaps, but English is a rich language. But a detective's time is not his own."

"Naturally. I might even say that a rabbi's time is not his own. This is the curse of a civilization that rushes so desperately. We must talk about Al Greenberg, may his soul rest in peace."

"He was a member of your congregation."

"In the most nominal sense. He was not a religious man—but pleasant and anxious to quiet his guilts with money. His contributions were generous, and when he married Phoebe three years ago, she decided to become Jewish. She was very grateful to him. Perhaps with reason. She was in the hospital, you know, with TB—in a ward, broke, two suicide attempts behind her. She had worked for him in what they call a 'special' some years before, and when he discovered she was in the hospital, he spared nothing to help her. The best doctors, the newest drugs—and then somehow he got up the nerve to ask her to marry him and she agreed. Gratitude. He endeared himself to her. But it was essentially a father-daughter relationship, no more than that. He was a widower. Of course, her becoming Jewish was not as serious as it might have been. I instructed her for two weeks and then her interest waned. But I got to know her a little—only why should this matter to the police?"

Detective Masuto told him why it mattered to the police, and the rabbi ate his yogurt and listened with interest, and then when Masuto finished, said, "I called the house when you telephoned me. Mrs. Greenberg was still asleep. I think I had better go over there now. She'll need someone to lean on.''

''You don't appear surprised.''

''At murder?'' asked Rabbi Gitlin. ''But you don't know that it is murder, and nothing should surprise us in this world.''

''I am not completely at home with the social relationships and overlaps of your Western religions, but would a man like Mr. Greenberg, under great stress, cry out the name of Jesus Christ?''

The rabbi shrugged. ''Who knows what any of us would do under great stress.''

''May I ask you an unspeakable question?''

''Of course,'' the rabbi smiled. ''But you must forgive me if I give you an unspeakable answer.''

''In your opinion, could Mrs. Greenberg have murdered her husband?''

''Not unspeakable, but interesting. You do not ask whether I think she had reason to, incitement to—but only whether she could have. But how could either of us, Detective Masuto, even know what the human mind and soul is capable of? Murder is a terrible ultimate. It is the ghost, the monster that lurks wherever human beings live. It is not your question that is unspeakable, but murder itself. I cannot accept the proposition that Al Greenberg was murdered, but if he was murdered, then that defines the murderer. You told me that you met Al Greenberg?''

''Several times.''

''Then you must understand that if he was murdered, then your murderer is without heart or compunction, someone who will stop at nothing. The very thought of such a murderer is particularly terrifying. I would be relieved if you told me your own thoughts.''

''That there was no murder?''

''I would like to think that, Detective Masuto.''

''Have you time enough for me to call Dr. Baxter—our

medical examiner? He should be at the hospital now, completing the autopsy."

"If you wish." The rabbi pointed to his telephone and Masuto dialed the hospital and was transferred to the autopsy room. A nurse answered and asked whether he would wait a moment or two, since Dr. Baxter was washing up. The rabbi watched Masuto thoughtfully. Then Baxter got on the phone and told him testily that he had spent three hours on a lot of nonsense.

"What did you find?" Masuto asked.

"That he died of a heart attack."

"Suppose—Doc, suppose that he fell down and someone held a pillow over his face for a minute or two. Would it show up in the autopsy?"

"No."

"Just like that?"

"Just like that. No. What do you want, an autopsy or the kind of nonsense you read in novels?"

"But the pillow would cause his death?"

"Well, of course it would. You don't breathe, you die."

"That would be murder."

"Not with me on the witness stand, it wouldn't. I told you he died of a myocardial infarction. That still goes."

"But the pillow?"

"I could invent a lot of other ways to kill him, and it would still be a heart attack. So you're on your own, my lad."

Mastuo replaced the telephone and turned to the rabbi, who smiled sadly. "I'm afraid I prefer to agree with your doctor," he said. "If you want a murder, Mr. Masuto, you must find it."

"Perhaps whether I want it or not, it'll find me."

"Perhaps."

In school, on being asked his mother's name—that is, her maiden name—Masuto's son had once replied, "Katherine

Asuki.'' Masuto was distressed when he heard about it, as he always was when he noticed any sense of action of inferiority on the part of his children. Her name was Kati or Katy, depending on how far the Anglicization went, and now Masuto pulled up at the loading walk of the Food Giant Supermarket, leaned out of the car and shouted, ''Hey, Kati—I'm here!''

It was one of the very few aggressive, extroverted actions he indulged in, and he only did it because he detested supermarkets. Now Kati came rushing out with her cart, exclaiming as always, ''Why do you embarrass me so? They will think we are people of no manners whatsoever.''

''Let them,'' he said, stowing the bags into the car. ''Come—in with you and off.'' She would not drive. He drove to his house and she apologized for interrupting his work so often.

''Today I have nothing to do,'' he said. ''The chief gave it to me. Today, tomorrow—so that he will be able to tell the press and everyone else that poor Mr. Greenberg died of a heart attack. If it had happened in Culver City or in Westwood or in Hollywood, that would be something else. Not in Beverly Hills—and least of all north of Wilshire Boulevard. So today I will prove there was no murder, and tomorrow I will go to the funeral and the next day we will all have a picnic at my uncle's farm.''

''That's very nice, but you're teasing me, aren't you?''

''No.''

''Where were you this morning?''

''With a rabbi,'' he said.

''A rabbi? That's a Jewish priest, isn't it?'' He burst out laughing, and she said plaintively, ''Why must you laugh at me? I don't pretend to know all these things. You knew I was an old-fashioned girl when you married me. Now you're sorry you married me.''

''If you are such an old-fashioned girl,'' he said, ''then why do you allow me to carry the bundles into the house?''

"Because I try to learn the things you teach me," she said sweetly.

The lady at the Screen Actors Guild had that quality of faded beauty that is so abundant in Hollywood and so occasional in the rest of the country. She was in her late sixties, Masuto judged, but with the bone structure of a star and the practiced dignity of at least a bit-part player. He seemed to remember having seen her in this film or that, and he wished he could refer to one of them with any certainty and thereby win her wholehearted cooperation. But he knew that if he faked a memory of her playing opposite Mary Pickford she would be insulted, and if he made it Joan Crawford, she would inform him that she had never been an actress. Things turned out that way for him.

When he showed her his badge, she studied him curiously and challengingly. It was plain that she did not approve of Oriental policemen or trust in geographic accidents of birth. Irritated a little, she wondered what she could do for him.

"You do keep membership records from year to year?"

"Not for the public," she informed him.

"I am not the public. I am Detective Sergeant Masuto, of the Beverly Hills Police Force. I told you that. I showed you my badge."

"Have you a warrant?"

"No, I have no warrant. I don't want to pry into your records. I want one simple fact. I want the address of an actress who may or may not belong to the Guild."

"This is Hollywood, not Beverly Hills. I think I should call the police here—"

"My dear lady," Masuto said softly, "I do not get angry or provoked, but if you insist on interfering, you will end up by being quite uncomfortable. Now listen to me. Eleven years ago, a girl called Samantha may or may not have joined this organization. I understand that you can play a speaking role once without joining, but then must join before the second job. Is that so?"

"Yes, and you might as well tell me her name."

"And yours, Miss?"

"Arthur."

"All right, Miss Arthur. Her name was Samantha."

"Samantha what?"

"I don't know. I have one name—Samantha."

"Then don't you think you ought to come back with the second name before you throw your weight around a poor, defenseless old lady?" she asked icily.

"I may or may not be able to find the second name. That is not your problem. I want every Samantha who joined the Guild eleven years ago, give or take a few months on either end. The name is not a common one and there can hardly be too many."

"Indeed!" said Miss Arthur.

"Indeed," Masuto smiled.

Whereupon Miss Arthur led him into another office where two girls sat, both of them younger even when their ages were added together, and where she figuratively washed her hands of Masuto.

"Who is she?" Masuto asked them. "I mean, who was she? The name sort of rings a bell."

"Della Arthur? And you didn't remember?" asked one.

"He didn't remember," said the other.

"She hates you. She'll cut your heart out. We'll let you out the back way, officer. We'll protect you."

"Are you married?"

"I'm married."

"Then we'll let her kill you. You know, all the Beverly Hills policemen are very handsome. Is that how they pick you?"

"I want—" Masuto began.

"We know," said one of them. "We heard. Enough of this light-hearted girlish talk. Only we don't file membership by year of admission. We file by name, and you don't have the family name.''

"But there must be some annual bookkeeping.''

"Oh, yes—yes. If she paid dues, we should have the receipts and the duplicate statements.'' The girl was dark haired and bright eyed, and she licked her lips when she looked at Masuto. "Why are they always married? Never mind. Come on, we'll go in the file room and study 1955 and we'll find a Samantha. Of course, you know that's a phony name,'' she said to Masuto.

She had led him into the next room, facing a whole wall of files, when he turned and looked at her curiously.

"Why do you say that, Miss—?''

"Just call me Jenny.''

"OK, Jenny. Why?''

"Well, isn't it obvious?''

"Not to my inscrutable Oriental mind. I grew up in a Japanese community, let us say a little apart from your folkways.''

"You know, Sergeant, you got a nice sense of humor. Cool, if you follow me.'' She had opened a file drawer and was riffling through it with practiced fingers as she spoke. "Suppose this Samantha is a kid of twenty or so in 1955. That makes her born in 1935, right?''

"Give or take a few years—yes.''

"Middle of the Depression—who's going to give a kid a nutty name like Samantha? Today's another matter, but around then, from what I hear, people weren't thinking about these stylish names.''

"Good. Go on.''

"I bet you a pretty penny her last name's a phony too.''

"How's that?''

"You know—like Glendale or Frazer or Buckingham or Sanford, but no Kaminski or Levy or Jones or Richter—''

"You'd make an excellent cop,'' Masuto said admiringly.

"Nah. Half the names here are phonies. It's part of the profession.''

"Do they also have to register their real names?"

"No rule about that. Some do. Most don't. If an actor takes a stage name, it becomes part of him. He usually can't live with two names. Hold on—here's a beginning. What do you know about that! Samantha Adams. Here's the address, on Sixth Street in Hollywood. That's a sorry block of bungalows turned rooming house a long time ago—so this kid was no millionaire."

Masuto copied down the name and address in his pad. There was no telephone number.

"No payment either," continued Jenny. "The large sum is for membership," she told Masuto, showing him the statement. "Almost two hundred with the dues, which is not hay by any means. You see, Sergeant, that's the initiation fee, entrance fee, lifetime. But it was never paid. Neither was the dues payment—that is, the first payment. Here's the follow-up statement and the second statement. That finishes the year. So this kid you're looking for never joined the Guild. She had one job, maybe two—but not three. I mean in the profession. Maybe she went back to slinging hash. That's another union. And she's the only one. No more Samantha's for 1955."

"You amaze me," Masuto nodded.

"You want me to amaze you some more, officer? I'm only doing it because you're the sexy type. I'll tell you something else about this kid. She never played anything real legitimate. Translated, that means adult theatre. She was never AEA."

"What's AEA?"

"Actors Equity. Legitimate theatre. Also, she was never AFTRA, which is TV and radio artists, and she never did the clubs—no stripping, no Las Vegas, not even the crumb joints. That's because she never claimed AGVA. So either she dumped it all—or else."

"How do you know all this?"

"No mystery. Look, we have this big overall membership fee of two hundred dollars. But there are also three

other major theatrical unions, and if one had to duplicate
the entrance fee for every membership, some of these kids
would die first. So we scale it. If you're an Equity member,
we give a credit of one hundred dollars. We also have a
code of notation for the statements. So that's how I do it.
And if your wife locks the door on you, give me a ring
right here. Nine to five. You just ask for Jenny. One
Samantha, one Jenny. I told you the last name would be a
phony too. Samantha Adams—get that.''

Out on Sunset Boulevard and walking toward his car,
Masuto wondered vaguely how it would be to be single and
to date someone like this Jenny. He had only dated a
Caucasian girl once, and she had been shapely but stupid.
It had not been a satisfactory evening at all. He was
impatient at himself for allowing his thoughts to wander. It
was wasteful and childish, and he gathered them together.

Sixth Street, east of Gower; it was an old, old Hollywood bungalow built of spit and slats, as they said, almost
half a century before, with the sign out, ''Furnished Rooms.
Transients Accommodated.'' In the old manner—the way
most California houses had been before air-conditioning—
the windows were closed and the blinds were drawn against
the hot noonday sun. Masuto rang the bell, and a fat,
frowzy woman of fifty or so, her feet in old slippers, her
ample body in a bathrobe and her breath alcoholic, opened
the door and said sourly. ''I know—you're a cop.''

''You've very perceptive.''

''Nuts. You got it written all over you, and I ain't
fooled by the Charlie Chan makeup. What do you want? I
run a clean, if a lousy house. Only men. This ain't no
Beverly Drive, so I don't want no hookers giving me
heartache.''

''I'm looking for a girl.''

''Then you're looking through the wrong keyhole, Officer Chan. I only rent to men.''

''That wasn't the case eleven years ago, I am sure.''

"Good God Almighty, nothing was the case eleven years ago. I was a hootchie-kootchie dancer eleven years ago, believe it or not. Sure, I took in a lady now and then in those days. But what do I remember? I ain't no elephant, except in appearance."

"This girl's name was Samantha Adams."

"Samantha Adams. You don't say."

"Maybe eighteen, twenty years old. Blue eyes, blond hair, good figure, maybe five feet six or seven inches tall—"

"Poor Officer Chan—what are you, an LA cop?"

"Beverly Hills," Masuto replied, taking out his billfold and showing her his badge.

"That accounts for it. Some day they give you a day off, wander along the Sunset Strip—you'll find maybe ten thousand babes to answer your description—no! No, wait a moment. Samantha Adams. That wasn't her real name. Some other name—no, I can't remember the other name for the life of me, but I remember her. I used to kid her about that Samantha business. Poor kid—poor, stupid kid."

"Why do you say that?" Masuto asked softly.

"Ah, she had no brains. You know, mister, for a dame this is the hardest, lousiest, dirtiest dark bunghole of a town in all these USA. Make it—you don't even exist out here unless you got a stainless steel ramrod up your you-know-where. This kid was soft—all the time soft and scared. Then one day she is going to lick the world and she goes off on a job at some studio—I think at World Wide, over in the Valley. Something happens. I don't know what—but here's a kid has the heart torn out of her. She has the curse after that, and we can't stop the bleeding, so I finally get a doctor and pay him. She comes out of it finally, but very weak and not good up on top. She's broke and a month behind. What the hell, I never threw a kid out on the street. That's why I stopped it with the dames. I know what it is to be one, and I ain't got the cabbage for an institution. So I don't even mention it to this Samantha kid, but one day she walks out. Leaves me her lousy suitcase and her few lousy clothes for payment—I should sell them. Can you imagine? Yes, sir, this world is one big joyride.''

"You said your name is Mrs. Baker?"

"Dolly Baker, sonny."

"You never saw her again?"

"No. That was 'Goodby Samantha.' "

"And you can't remember her name—the other name?"

"It'll come to me."

"You wouldn't have a register or anything like that?"

"Buster," she smiled, "what do I look like, a sap? They can make their spaceships without my poor widow's mite."

He grinned back at her. "Thanks, Mrs. Baker. You have great heart, and I think that when you reflect on it and realize that I bear no harm for this poor girl, you will remember. Here's my card. Will you call me when the name comes back to you?"

"Masao Masuto," she read from the card. "I like you, buster. I'll call you, but if that poor kid is in something that stinks, find the lousy male bastard that put her there and go easy on her. Will you?"

"I'll try, Mrs. Baker."

"You're Leo, aren't you?" she asked, looking at him narrowly.

"How did you know?" He was impressed but not astounded, recalling that he had shown her the open wallet with badge and identity card.

"I'm sensitive to such things. I am Scorpio myself— very perceptive. That girl didn't steal anything. She did not hurt anyone. You take my word for that."

"It's eleven years later."

"People don't change—not the deep nut of them. You ought to know that, Officer Chan."

CHAPTER THREE

Murphy Anderson

It was just 12:15, just past midday, when Detective Sergeant Masuto parked his car behind one of the new savings and loan office buildings on Wilshire Boulevard in Beverly Hills. Northeastern Films had the entire sixth floor, with at least one hundred thousand dollars worth of modern-Italian-Southern-California decor; but today the bright edge of wealth was muted by the haze of death. The men and women who worked in the offices of Northeastern were depressed by the fact that it was incumbent upon them to be depressed by the death of Al Greenberg.

The girl at the reception desk looked upon Masuto bleakly as he told her that he had an appointment with Mr. Anderson. She spoke into the phone and then she rose and led Masuto through a section of minor offices at the rear of the floor. This whole end of the floor was divided into three offices. According to the names on the door, the center office belonged to Al Greenberg, the one on the left to John D. Cotter, and the one on the right to Murphy Anderson.

Expressionless faces examined them as they walked through, and when they reached Anderson's office, the big, white-haired man opened the door himself, invited Masuto to be seated, and closed the door behind him. Masuto lowered himself into a straight-backed Italian import, and Anderson applogized for not having Cotter there with them.

"You don't know what this has done to us, Sergeant. Jack's been at the bank all morning, and that's only the beginning. I have been talking to five hundred people and trying to help Phoebe arrange the funeral proceedings at the same time." He looked at his watch. "As a matter of fact, I have a very important luncheon meeting at one. I imagine we can finish by then. I have been talking to your boss at the police station, and he agrees that there is absolutely no sense in pursuing the murder angle. We have no evidence of murder, no real suspicion of anyone, and a very definite knowledge of poor Al's illness. Jack Cotter is willing to forget what he heard. Do you agree?"

"It hardly matters whether I agree or not," Masuto said, spreading his hands slightly. "Mine is a negative search—simply to dispel any lingering doubts. I think the very fact that this was kept out of the papers helps your desire."

"Thank God for that. I don't mind telling you—but in confidence—that we are in the middle of the biggest move in the history of this business, the acquisition of the remaining library of World Wide Films—for eighteen million dollars. Jack Cotter finished signing the papers this morning. If this had broken as murder, the deal would have been postponed or killed completely."

"Then if we were fanciful," Masuto smiled, "we could say that the murderer attempted to frustrate your deal."

"Then why didn't she break the story to the press?"

Masuto shrugged. "Who knows? Could you tell me something, perhaps, about your company."

"To what point?"

"Again—who knows? But I am curious. If I am not mistaken, Mr. Greenberg began the company some fifteen years ago?"

"Closer to twelve years. He and I began together, and then we took Jack Cotter in. Al began to produce TV shows about fifteen years ago. He was one of the first. I was his lawyer, and he organized the company to produce and I went in with him. But I don't take any credit. I am a lawyer and a businessman, a good lawyer and a pretty good businessman, but I think I would make a lousy producer. Whatever Northeastern is, Al Greenberg is mainly responsible.''

''How did Jack Cotter come into it?''

''Jack was a sort of Western star back in the late 'thirties. He made five feature films for Asterlux, and they went bankrupt in 1940—or almost bankrupt. They liquidated their assets and settled. They owed Jack a hundred thousand dollars in back wages, and as a settlement they gave him the American distribution rights to the five Westerns. Who ever knew then how TV would eat feature films! Back in 1957, Jack proposed to throw his five features into our operation in return for a piece of stock and a vice-presidency in the company. We needed the features and we took him in.''

''Is Sidney Burke also in the firm?''

''Not exactly in it. He began with our publicity right from the beginning. He's good. At first he worked almost for nothing. Then he got some stock. He still does our publicity, but he has his own company.''

''Would you mind telling me who the stockholders are?''

''Why?''

''Because it would be easier if you told me,'' Masuto said, ''than if I had to track down the information. I could, you know.''

''You still want to make something out of this, don't you?''

''No. What is there, is there, Mr. Anderson. If nothing is there—''

''OK. There are five stockholders—or were. Al held sixteen thousand shares. His wife, Phoebe, five thousand, a gift from him when they were married. Sidney has two thousand and Jack has four thousand. I own six thousand shares, which makes me the second largest stockholder."

"And Mr. Tulley—Mike Tulley?"

"He has no shares. Why should he? We hired him three years ago and we made him a TV star. But at this point our shares have a book value of almost three hundred dollars each. There's no market on them, but if there were, it would be enormous."

"And now what happens to Mr. and Mrs. Greenberg's shares?"

"Nothing happens to Phoebe's—unless she decides to sell. And I have advised her not to and I will continue to so advise her. But Al's personal stock, according to our initial agreement, goes back into the company treasury, and his estate is paid fifty percent of book value. Providing Jack and I refuse to purchase."

"How's that?"

"If any one of the three officers dies, the remaining two have the right to divide his stock and purchase it at twenty-five percent of book value. The remaining twenty-five percent is then paid by the company treasury. It's a peculiar arrangement, but perfectly legal and it protects the officers and major stockholders."

"And what do you and Mr. Cotter intend to do?"

"We'll buy the stock, of course. Are you thinking of that as a motive? But whose motive for Al's death, Sergeant? I am the only one who profits. I gain control, God help me. There's no reason for you to believe me, but I'd blow this business and ten like it to give Al a week of extra living."

"We were not to talk of murder, but simply to eliminate any possibility of it. Forgive me if I raise a rather shameful matter, Mr. Anderson, but do you remember an incident with a girl called Samantha? Eleven years ago?"

Murphy Anderson stared at Masuto for a long moment. Then he swung on his heel and walked to the window. When he turned back, his face was cold and set.

"What the hell business is that of yours, Sergeant?"

"Last night, Mike Tulley asked me to come over. He told me about the incident. He was very frightened. I gathered that he is under the impression that one of you— one of your four men, or five if we include Greenberg—is married to Samantha."

"Let me tell you something about Al Greenberg, Sergeant. I never spoke of this until now. But Al never touched that kid. I'm not defending myself or Jack or Mike or Sidney. What we are, we are. But Al went into that dressing room, looked at the kid, had a few words with her and came out. He was the last. Don't worry—I remember, I goddamn well remember. Jack had disappeared, and when Sidney saw Al's face, he took off. Al said to me, 'If anything like this ever happens again on one of my sets, Murph, I will kill you and everyone else concerned with my own hands. And I'm not kidding. You were high in my esteem, and now you are low as a turd—you and that stinking shithead Sidney.' Maybe not those exact words, but that was the tune."

"Then if what you say is true," Masuto said slowly, "why are we all quietly thinking that Samantha murdered him?"

"Baloney. Why would she wait eleven years?"

"Then would you mind telling me the gist of your discussion with Mr. Cotter, concerning Samantha?"

"I would mind. It has no bearing here."

"Have you also spoken to Sidney Burke about it?"

"You know, I don't like those questions, Sergeant Masuto. Not one goddamn bit. Your job is to protect the citizens of this community, not to harass them. I am no stranger at City Hall—"

"You know well enough what my job is, Mr. Anderson. You are an officer of the court, so don't threaten me. I don't threaten you. This case is sticky as flypaper, and my hands are full of it and I am trying to walk a tightrope at the same time. I ask you something, and you could blow your top and slug me, and what would that solve?''

''I don't blow my top. So if you got any questions, ask them and then get to hell out of here!''

''Do you believe your wife is Samantha?'' Masuto asked flatly.

Anderson's face whitened and he clenched his fists. He took a step toward Masuto, and then his telephone rang. He picked it up, shouted into it, ''I told you, no calls!'' and slammed it back into its cradle. It rang again. He picked it up and listened. The white of his face became whiter.

''Oh, my God,'' he said. ''My God—my God.''

He put the telephone down and stared hopelessly at Masuto.

''What happened?'' Masuto asked him.

''Mike Tulley has just been murdered. Shot. With his wife's gun.''

There were cars all around the Tulley house. This one had not been kept quiet. There were newspapermen at the place and more still arriving. Over a dozen cars were crowded in and around the driveway.

Officer Frank Seaton supervised the half-dozen uniformed men who were trying to keep the newspaper people and the curious out of the house—and at the same time keep the traffic moving on Benedict Canyon Road. Inside the house, Detective Beckman was in charge. They were waiting for Masuto to arrive before they removed the body, and Beckman immediately led Masuto into the study. Murphy Anderson stayed in the living room. Anderson remained silent. Like so many big, fleshy men, a mood could age him. He had not spoken a word on the way over with Masuto, and he said nothing now as he slumped into a chair in the living room.

''Why?'' asked Detective Beckman, nodding at him.

"He's the boss now," Masuto said. "I want him here. Something's going on inside him that I don't know about."

Beckman closed the door of the study behind them—the same room Masuto had been in the night before, except that now it was full of smoke form Dr. Sam Baxter's cigar. There were also the fingerprint man, the photographer and two men from the hospital, Beverly Hills being too small a community to boast its own police autopsy facilities. The mortal remains of Mike Tulley lay on the floor, covered by a thin rubber sheet, which Dr. Baxter callously threw back. Tulley's body was stripped to the waist. There were three small, ugly bullet holes in his chest.

"There you are, Masao," said Baxter. "Close range. Thirty-two lady's gun. Smith and Wesson automatic. Victim died of heart failure but not of a heart attack."

"Your sense of humor leaves something to be desired," Masuto said. "God help him."

"Macabre job, macabre humor. I don't get too many murders, Masao, but they mash themselves up in cars day in and day out. Half the human race is in a frenzied race to eliminate itself. Can we take him away?"

Masuto nodded, and the hospital attendants put the body on a stretcher and carried it out.

"What about them?" Beckman asked, motioning to fingerprints and photography.

"They should be finished now."

Reluctantly, the fingerprint man and the photographer allowed themselves to be ushered out of the room. Dr. Baxter dropped into a chair and relit his cigar. Detective Beckman seated himself on the built-in couch. Masuto remained standing, staring at the blood blot on the carpet. Tall, sliding aluminum doors at one side of the study opened onto planting and swimming pool—that heady badge of status that is almost obligatory in Beverly Hills. The contained vista was very beautiful, and Masuto thought he recognized the work of Hono Asaki, the landscape gardener who was very much in demand at the moment. Standing there, Masuto attempted to feel something of what the dead man had felt. It was not good to die in the face of such beauty—in youth and vigor. But then, it is not good to die, anywhere, anyplace.

Beckman rose, went to the table, and picked up a cardboard box. It contained the gun.

"You want to look at this, Masao?"

"Her gun?"

"Right."

"She admits it?"

"Right."

"Send it over to ballistics. Where is she?"

"Upstairs, lying down. She was hysterical. Doc gave her something to quiet her down."

"What did you give her?" Masuto asked Baxter.

"A placebo. Two aspirin. No shock, just lady hysterics. She quieted down almost immediately."

"You're a witch doctor," Beckman said.

"Aren't we all?"

"Do you want to see her now?" asked Beckman.

"Later. Tell me about it. It seems I make a practice of coming in after everyone else is seated."

"As long as you're on time for the next one. As far as we can put it together, this is it. According to the wife. She's the only witness. The lady who did the killing—"

"Lady?"

"So it would seem. I am giving you Mrs. Tulley's version, because it's the only version we got. This lady killer, who seems to be the coldest dish around this town, evidently parked her car down the road toward Lexington. One of our cops saw it there when he was making his rourds, but he didn't give it a second glance. It was a cream-colored car, he thinks, but it could be dull yellow, and it could be either a Pontiac, an Olds or a Buick, or maybe just something that looks like one of them. That's what you train a cop for, to be observant. Well, she walked up to the driveway, and either Tulley let her into the house himself or she came around here and in through the windows. They have a housekeeper, who was in the kitchen. They have a maid, who was upstairs. Maybe Tulley knew she was coming. Anyway from when the cop saw the car, we guess that this killer-type broad arrived here about noon or thereabouts. Ten or fifteen minutes later, Mrs. Tulley comes down. She is dressed and on her way to make a lunch date at the Beverly Wilshire. The lunch date is a Susie Cohn, and we checked that out because she called here to see what was keeping Lenore. But Mrs. Tulley has to have a word with her husband before she leaves the house and she comes to the study, tries the door, finds it locked. 'Mike!' she calls out. 'Open up.' Then she hears a woman's voice, 'The mills of the gods, you—' ''

At this point, Detective Beckman consulted his notebook.

''Yeah, this is it, 'The mills of the gods, you dirty louse!' Then Tulley yells, 'What are you talking like that for? Are you nuts? Put away that gun!' Then three shots, deliberate, one, two, three. Then the sound of Tulley's body hitting the floor. Then Mrs. Tulley begins to scream. The cook comes running. The maid comes running. There is Mrs. Tulley screaming and pounding on the door. They think they hear a car start—but it doesn't send any message to them. Then the maid gets the idea to run around to the big sliding windows. As she leaves the house, she sees Tulley's car swing out of the driveway to the right. It's parked on Benedict Canyon Road, where the killer picked up her own car and drove off, just as cool as a cucumber. Apparently, she knocked off Tulley and then walked through the sliding doors into the garden, like a lady should, got into Tulley's car and took off.''

''Fingerprints on the gun?''

''Are you kidding?'' Beckman said.

''What do you think?''

''What should I think? If Mrs. Tulley let him have it,

how did she get around to the other side of a locked door
in all of ten seconds, and who drove Tulley's car out and
down almost to Lexington? They all seem to have heard
the car start, and the maid saw it swing out of the driveway.
Mrs. Tulley left the maid upstairs so that accounts for her.
The cook is an old Mexican lady, and Doc had to give her
the real thing, not a placebo. So what is left?''

"Speculation," Masuto said thoughtfully. "Fascinating
speculation."

"You put the two broads together?" Beckman asked.

"At least the two deaths," Masuto replied. "The poor
chief wanted so desperately not to have a murder in
Beverly Hills."

"Come in," Lenore Tulley said in reply to Masuto's
knock. She was not in bed, but sitting by the window,
fully dressed and smoking a cigarette. Unlike the rest of
the house, Mrs. Tulley's bedroom was aggressively
nonmodern, with a mahogony four-poster bed, a large
hooked rug, dotted Swiss curtains, and two very fine and
expensive early American chests. While Masuto's knowledge of furniture and decor was by no means encyclope-
dic or wholly discriminating, he was possessed of good
taste and he recognized that while the room was odd, or at
least at odds with the rest of the house, it was neither
vulgar nor pretentious.

"My hair used to be brown," Lenore Tulley said evenly.
"I graduated Smith, class of '56. I am not a bona fide
California product, and the furniture in this room was in
my room in Connecticut when I was a kid. I am frightened
but not grief-stricken, Sergeant. Let me make that plain. It
is an ugly thing—and very upsetting too—to have your
husband murdered while you are forced to stand on the
wrong side of a locked door and do nothing about it.
Believe me, if it were possible, I would have saved my
husband's life. I disliked him intensely, but I had no desire
to see him murdered. If I do any weeping, it is only for

myself. One never really recovers from a murder, does one?"

"That all depends," Masuto said, smiling slightly. "The victim never recovers, does he? The murderer sometimes recovers, I suppose. The innocent bystander—well—tell me, if you disliked Mike Tulley so, why did you remain married to him?"

She shrugged. "That's almost too complex to unravel. We separated twice. I am very wealthy—much more than he—but more recently. My father died last year, and I inherited a great deal. There's a community property law in this state. I was not in love with anyone else. I am neurotic as hell and I see an analyst five times a week, and in this rotten social blister called Los Angeles, there's a certain value in being married to a TV star. There's no other status out here. Also, Mike made a divorce a rough thing—"

"Then generally speaking, his death benefits and liberates you," Masuto said softly, not knowing what reaction this would evoke from her.

But she only shrugged and nodded. "If you want to look at it that way. I suppose poor Mike made it a little easier for me. I don't know."

"And the murder—can you talk about it now?"

"Why not?"

"Dr. Baxter said you were hysterical."

"So I was upset. That idiot doctor of yours gave me a couple of aspirin. He partakes of a general Beverly Hills belief in the stupidity of women. I'm all right now."

"As I understand it, you were on your way out to make a luncheon date and you knocked at the door of the study. You were coming from upstairs?"

"That's right."

"From this room?"

"Yes."

"How long had you been here in this room?"

"About an hour—dressing, makeup. My maid, Binnie,

was with me—not to help me dress, I can dress perfectly well by myself and I prefer to. But Binnie had a fight yesterday with some stupid kid she's dating, and she was crying on my shoulder.''

"You left her in the room when you went out?''

"No, she followed me out on the landing and began to whine about what should she do.''

"Giving you an absolutely perfect alibi," Masuto reflected.

"Well, don't hate me for that, Sergeant. No one will believe it. By tonight, everyone will have made up his or her mind that I killed poor Mike.''

"I don't think so. Now, you knocked on the door. Did you hear the woman's voice immediately?''

"No, there was an interval of silence. I suppose you could count ten. Then that crazy voice.''

"Crazy? Why crazy?''

"That's it. I don't know.''

"But you said crazy voice. Why?''

"Because it was different, I suppose. A high, hysterical voice. It shook and trembled. I just never heard a voice like that before.''

"Then it did not remind you of anyone you know?''

"Maybe. I am not sure.''

"Look, Mrs. Tulley, either it did remind you or it did not. Which is it?''

"It reminded me. It reminded me of someone's voice.''

"Who's?''

"I don't know.''

"Dear lady, please. Be reasonable. If it reminded you of a voice, you must know who it reminded you of.''

"I don't.''

"All right. Was the voice mocking? Hateful?''

"Mocking, I would say.''

"And your husband's voice?''

"Afraid. Oh, my God, he was so afraid—you know, I can't feel any grief and yet it breaks my heart. He was so afraid." She began to cry and went over to one of the chests for a fresh handkerchief.

"Are you all right?" Masuto asked.

"Quite. Go on, please. I want to see the bitch who did this drawn and quartered. Why? What gave her the right? Because a man's a louse? If you go around killing every man who is a louse to some dame, then you'll end the male population, period! I hate her. Tulley—Tulley was just a permanent adolescent, an all-American boy who never grew up, just like every other all-American boy. Why did she kill him? He wasn't even a real, high-class louse. He was only a slob, a good-looking TV slob."

"What bitch?" Masuto asked. "Samantha?"

She studied him narrowly for a moment. "What do you know about Samantha?"

"A bit here. A bit there. What do you know about her?"

She cried a bit again, and then she dried her eyes and said, "I wish I was like you, Sergeant."

"How is that?"

"Japanese. Out of it. So I could stand back and look at it. You must get some kind of special kick out of looking at a sewer."

"I live in the same sewer," Masuto said. "Also, I'm a Nisei. Here I am and here I live. I would like to talk about Samantha."

"Oh, I just bet you would!"

"Will you?"

"You are damn right I will. Talk and anything else that will put a rope around that bitch's neck. Shall I tell you something, Mr. Detective? I had not seen my father for two years, but when he died it was the worst thing that ever happened to me until now. Maybe worse, because I loved him and I could never break down the wall between us. Do you know who I ran to the day he died?"

"Al Greenberg?"

"That's right, Al Greenberg. And that rotten bitch murdered Al Greenberg and now she murdered Mike."

"When did you find out about Samantha?"

"Last night. After you left. It was a stinking, dirty mess, just the way this whole thing is. I don't know how to tell it to you."

"Any way. Try. I'm not a human being. I'm a cop."

"He accused me of being Samantha, Sergeant. Can you imagine? He accused me of being Samantha."

"Well, that's not so strange. He was overwrought, terrified, filled with guilt. Did you know about Samantha at that point? When he accused you?"

"No. I did not. Furthermore, I made him understand that when he and his anthropoid buddies were having their gangshag, I was in Smith College in western Massachusetts. And then that fool—that poor fool had the nerve to ask me whether I could prove it."

"Then you know what had happened to Samantha?"

"No. Not then. I'm mixing up the sequence last night— that's because I'm upset."

"I understand," Masuto said. "He accused you of being Samantha, but you did not know what he meant?"

"Exactly. I said to him, 'Mike, are you nuts?' Oh, I was no joy. I hate myself. But I did not know he was going to be killed. I said, 'Mike, I always knew you were a louse, but I always figured you for a louse with marbles. Do I have to tell you that I am your own miserable, everloving wife, Lenore? Smith College, class of '56. Have you really flipped? Haven't you looked at my yearbook? What kind of a nut are you? And who is this Samantha?' Then he wanted out of the whole thing, but I wouldn't let go. Then he told me. I think he enjoyed telling me."

"The dressing room, the part in a TV show, the arrangements that Sidney Burke made?"

"Right down the line. Oh, he was a daisy, my Mike— right down the line. Do you mind if I have a drink?"

"Go ahead."

"Will you join me?"

Masuto shook his head. Lenore Tulley went to a cedar chest, opened it and by that motion caused a small but well-equipped bar to rise out of its depths. She poured herself a straight vodka and threw it down her throat.

"You're sure you won't join me?" she asked Masuto again. "You know—you're a good-looking cop. How old are you?"

"Old enough not to drink in a lady's bedroom while I am on duty."

"How about that? Shouldn't you have a stenographer in here taking notes and all that?"

"No. You're not a suspect—"

Detective Sy Beckman knocked on the door, and then entered. "Masao," he said, "what about the news boys talking to Mrs. Tulley? Also the CBS and ABC and NBC trucks are outside. They all want Mrs. Tulley."

Masuto looked inquiringly at Lenore Tulley, who shook her head and said, "I have had it. They can drop dead, the lot of them. Los Angeles, farewell. They can get lost in the smog."

"You'll have to talk to them sooner or later," Beckman said.

"Then later."

"Tell them she is prostrated and unable to talk to anyone."

"No!" she exclaimed.

"Tell them that," Masuto said.

Beckman left, and Lenore Tulley said to Masuto, "You got a hell of a lot of nerve for a—"

"For a Jap?"

"Just don't push me around. I have had enough of being pushed around."

Masuto rose abruptly and started for the door.

"Where are you going?" she demanded.

"To look for whoever killed your husband, instead of pushing you around."

"Oh, stop being a horse's ass and sit down," she said. "I never met a male who didn't have all the engaging tactics of a frustrated six-year-old. You're married, right?"

"Right."

"I never met a decent man who wasn't. Only the slobs are *libres*."

"*Libres?*"

"That's what they call the cabs in Mexico. It means they're free for customers."

"Murphy Anderson is sitting down in your living room."

"Let him sit. You keep testing, don't you?"

"That's what they pay me for, Mrs. Tulley—"

"Call me Lenore. You've moved into my bedroom." She poured herself another vodka and tossed it down, shivered, and said to Masuto, "What are you, anyway? I mean, Christian or Mormon or ancestor worship or what?"

"I am a Buddhist, Mrs. Tulley. You've been married six years. No children?"

"That is none of your damn business. Christ, maybe it is. I don't know what is your business. I was married to Mike. You know, he kept a little book of every dame he took to bed, one hundred and twenty-seven entries, names, places, dates and physical descriptions, just in case he should confuse them."

"He showed it to you?"

"No, my dear Detective Masuto. I got at it when he was away. Dirty curiosity. And you want me to have kids with that? Oh, no—thank God, that's one I missed." She stared at him then with awakened interest. "Good Lord, you still think that maybe I am Samantha, don't you?"

"No, you're not Samantha. But suppose we take four of your friends, Mrs. Tulley—Trude Burke, Phoebe Greenberg, Stacy Anderson and Arlene Cotter—"

"My friends?"

"You know them well, don't you?"

"What is well? Arlene Cotter is a bitch with the mouth of a snake. Stacy folds her hands across her belly and she drinks too much. She's contented Bevery Hills. Phoebe Greenberg—well, no one knows her. I don't even think Phoebe knows her. The day after she married Al, she became Great Lady of Beverly Hills. It's the only part she ever had and she decided she would play it better without any speaking lines. And Trude Burke is a little tramp.''

"Oh? What do you mean when you call someone a tramp?''

She downed a third vodka and replied, "I mean I'm being a bitch. And if you don't know what a tramp is, my inscrutable Oriental, look it up in Mencken on slang.''

"And which of the four is Samantha, Mrs. Tulley?''

"You must be kidding.''

"Not at all. Will you answer a question truthfully—one question?''

"You're impugning me, and I no longer like you, Mr. Chan. I know damn well what you intend to ask me. You are going to say, 'My dear Mrs. Tulley, is one of them Samantha?' The answer is yes. One of them is Samantha. You're goddamn right one of them is!''

"Which one?''

Lenore Tulley shook her head. She was a little drunk and she was becoming thoughtful.

"Which one?''

"Fuzz,'' she answered with distaste. "What am I doing here in my own bedroom with an Oriental fuzz playing psychological games with me? Drop dead, Mr. Detective.''

"You said you wanted to get your husband's killer.''

"Did I? What could I have been thinking of? Killing Mike was a public service. She deserves a medal.''

In the bedlam downstairs, Murphy Anderson sat like a lost child, hunched over in his chair, warding off the reporters and hiding from the TV cameras, which were still barred from the house.

Masuto watched him as Beckman said, "Do you want to talk to the maid, housekeeper?''

"No. Get their statements."

"There's no one you want to arrest?" Beckman asked hopefully.

"No—no one."

"Let me get out of here, would you?" Murphy Anderson asked.

"You don't want to talk to the widow?"

"No, I don't want to talk to the widow. I only want to get out of here."

"All right," Masuto nodded. "I think I have had enough of this place too. I'll drive you over to your office. Now remember, they will crawl all over you when you leave here. Just walk straight ahead with me. Say nothing."

"I'm a lawyer," Anderson growled.

"Of course you are. How stupid of me!"

Out in the sunshine, they pushed past reporters, the curious, and the TV people. A cop came alongside of Masuto and said softly, "They got a call downtown from a Mrs. Baker. She wants you should drop by and talk to her."

"All right. I'll get to it."

He got Murphy Anderson to his car and into it, and then they were worming their way through the traffic, down Benedict Canyon Drive to Sunset. Anderson lay back in his seat, his eyes closed.

"How stupid of me," Masuto repeated. "Forgetting that you are a lawyer and asking you whether you thought your wife was Samantha. A nasty question, and an invitation to give evidence against your wife."

"Evidence? What the hell, nothing I say to you means anything in a court!"

"And what does Tulley's death do to your company?"

"It's a blow. It's a shot in the belly. It means that the show is over. No more 'Lonesome Rider.' Well, we're insured—I mean Mike was insured in our favor."

"How much?"

"A quarter of a million dollars."

"That's a comfort, isn't it?"

"It's a comfort, as you say, but we're still in the red. We lose a lot more than a quarter of a million."

"Well, to a cop such numbers have no practical meaning. I do apologize for an inconsiderate question. But tell me, please, who do you think is Samantha?"

"Now that's nicely put, isn't it, Sergeant? Who do I think is Samantha? I can tell you who Samantha is—she's a little tramp who bit off more than she could chew. I'm sick of all this weeping over a stupid kid who invites disaster. But who is Samantha? The answer is no one. This whole Samantha kick is a phony."

"Then you don't think Samantha murdered Tulley?"

"I do not."

"And you don't think that one of your associates might be married to Samantha?"

"Nuts."

They were at Wilshire now. Masuto said that he would like to come up to the offices for just a moment. Anderson protested only a bit.

"The whole world has fallen in. There are only twelve hundred things for me to do, Sergeant. Why don't you give me a break for today."

"Murderers are always inconsiderate. But Detective Beckman tells me that Cotter is in the office, and I would like to have a word with him."

But it turned out that Cotter had been there and left.

"Did he say where he was going?" Anderson asked his secretary.

"I imagined he was going over to poor Mr. Tulley's home."

"When was that?"

"At least a half hour ago. I had two ham-on-ryes and two coffees sent up. They're inside. The coffee is still warm. I felt that perhaps you would not have time to eat."

"You felt right," Anderson replied, leading Masuto into his office.

The sandwiches were on a tray on his desk. "Actually, they are ham and cheese. The world caves in, but you go on eating—especially when you're a compulsive eater. That's my problem. You know, I'm becoming fond of you, Sergeant. That snotty Oriental manner is intriguing. How about I put you in a TV pilot? We got to have something to replace the 'Lonesome Rider,' who's plenty lonesome now, believe me. Ever thought of being an actor?"

"Who hasn't?" Masuto smiled. "It's the occupational daydream of Los Angeles. I have a cousin who works all the time. He's that heavy-set, sadistic general who always sits at a table eating, and says, 'Take American out, shoot him.' My wife's sister was in the Brando film."

"Have a sandwich."

"I am honored," Masuto said, taking the sandwich gratefully. He was starved. He bit into it and chewed thoughtfully and then said, "Didn't anyone like Tulley?"

"Everyone loved him. He received over a thousand letters a week—fans. They adored him. In Chicago, they tore off his pants."

"Just between you and me, Mr. Anderson—who do you think killed him?"

"Have some coffee."

"Of course," Masuto said, accepting the coffee, "that's the trouble with this case. Every one of you knows who the killer is. Maybe the candidate isn't the same in every case, but you all know. Only, there's one thing you apparently can't get into your respective skulls—that this killer is a homicidal maniac, and that he will kill again and again and again."

"That's your guess."

"No. That's the way the symbols are arranged—but you don't believe in symbols anymore, and you don't see them. You are a people enlightened—"

The loudspeaker intercom on Anderson's desk crackled

at that moment, and his secretary said, "I have a call for Detective Sergeant Masuto."

"Any name?" Masuto asked.

"Oh, yes. She said you would know her. Her name is Samantha."

Anderson reached for the phone, but Masuto gripped his arm and said quickly, "Do you have a private line in the office?"

"There, in the corner," pointing to a phone on an end table next to the couch.

"Get on it. Call the operator. Use my name, give her the main number, and trace us. Quick."

Then, as Anderson ran across the room to the other phone, Masuto lifted the one on the desk and said, "Hello. This is Sergeant Masuto."

"All right, Masuto—this is Samantha. Now listen carefully. I am not going to repeat." The voice was the precise, controlled, theatrically trained voice of a professional.

"Now wait a minute. Let me get my pad."

"Come off it, Masuto. I know you're having the call traced right now. That will take you at least eleven minutes. I don't propose to give you more than five."

"You're optimistic if you think we can trace a call in eleven minutes. How do I know you're Samantha?"

"How? Because I know what went on in that lousy trailer room when that little louse, Sidney Burke, arranged for his gangshag."

"A good many ladies seem to know," Masuto said.

"No, no. Not at all. Let me give you the rundown, Sergeant. Max Green was in that room, and he's dead—"

"Who is Max Green?" Masuto interrupted.

"Interrupt me once more, mister, and I hang up. Now are you ready to listen?"

"Go ahead."

"Max Green was there, and he's dead. A rotten little creep called Fred Saxton was there, and he's dead. Al Greenberg was there and he's dead. Mike Tulley was there, and he's dead. Which leaves Jack Cotter, Murphy Anderson and Sidney Burke. Four down, three to go. You know, Sergeant, just to convince that heathen and doubting Oriental mind of yours, the gun that killed Mike Tulley was a thirty-two-caliber Smith and Wesson. It was his wife's gun. I shot him three times in the chest. None of that has been on the air yet. Check me and see. As for the other three— tell them to expect me.''

She hung up, and Masuto replaced the phone and said to Anderson, ''Let it go, Mr. Anderson. She's off.''

''Was it Samantha?'' he asked eagerly.

''That's what she said.''

''What else did she say?''

Almost word for word, Masuto repeated what the woman had said—all of it, leaving nothing out, and watching Murphy Anderson's face as he spoke. At the end, he said to Anderson, ''Who is Fred Saxton and who is Mike Green?''

''Oh, my God,'' Anderson whispered.

''Who are they?''

''Fred Saxton was the production manager on the 'Lonesome Rider.' Max Green was the assistant producer.''

''Isn't that sort of the same job?''

''Sort of.''

''Then I presume they're both dead?''

''Yes, they're dead. We had changed the title from assistant producer to production manager and then we gave the job to Fred Saxton.''

''How did they die, Mr. Anderson?''

''Max died a normal death. My God, this thing is insane enough without making it crazier. Max died of a heart attack, over a year ago.''

''How old was he?''

''I don't know—forty-six, forty-seven.''

''Then it wasn't so normal, was it?''

''Why? It's young, but people die of heart attacks in their forties. It happens.''

"And how did Fred Saxton die?"

"One of these stupid accidents—" He broke off, rose suddenly, and went to a little bar in the room and poured himself a glass of brandy.

"You want a little brandy, Sergeant?"

"No. So maybe it was not an accident. What happened?"

Anderson drank the brandy, wincing and making faces. "His skull was crushed. On one of the sound stages we rent over at World Wide. A hundred-pound sandbag counterweight fell from the beam where it was rigged. He never knew what hit him. Died instantly. Terrible—just terrible."

"I thought everything was lead counterweights and electric winches today."

"This was an old stage. Those bags could have been up there for years—I don't know. But it could have been an accident too."

"I suppose so," Masuto admitted.

"Can I tell Jack and Sidney about what she said?"

"Why not? A few minutes ago, you refused to give an inch about our Semantha. Have you changed your mind?"

"I don't know," Anderson replied.

CHAPTER FOUR

Peggy Groton

When Masuto entered City Hall on Santa Monica Boulevard, he was already aware of a glow of notoriety in which the city would alternately squirm and bask. Beverly Hills was hardly a place for violent murder. He sometimes thought of the place as a toy city, with a toy police force to guard people who dreamed away their lives, but those were very private thoughts and not proper to any bona fide policeman. Usually, he came and went unnoticed, but today reporters tried to buttonhole him, and curious ones, town bureaucrats and employees, begged to be let in on the facts.

His chief also begged. "What I want to know, Masao, is do the two deaths connect? Do we have some kind of a double killing on our hands?"

"Maybe a triple killing," Masuto said. "This is one with a taste for blood and death. This is a demon. But you don't believe in demons, do you?"

"I also do not buy any high-class Oriental philosophy at this moment. I also don't like a cop who gets on a connecting bug and goes off on a mass-killer kick. Just before you came in, it was on the wire that some dame goes off Mulholland Drive on the alley side. You'll connect that up too."

"What dame?"

"I don't know. It's Hollywood anyway. Haven't we got enough trouble? Let the city worry about it."

"Who's up there?"

"I don't know, rescue service and city cops, I suppose. What's the difference?"

"Did the car burn?"

"How do I know if the car burned?"

"Chief, do me a favor," Masuto said, trying to control his excitement. "Believe me—something is happening, something is working out. Get them on the radiophone and tell them to hold everything until I get there. Not to touch the car. I don't mean they should not take the woman to the hospital—"

"The woman's dead, Saito."

"Of course—of course. Will you phone them?"

"They're city cops—all right, I'll phone. I had to go and hire a Japanese cop. But what about all this? Where are we? Was All Greenberg murdered?"

"He was murdered."

"You're sure?"

"No one's ever sure about such a killing."

"And Tulley?"

"The same killer. That's a very strong opinion. More opinion is that the same civilized joker murdered a third man, one Fred Saxton, on the World Wide lot about seven weeks ago. Perhaps a fourth man—that waits to be seen. And nothing is going to wish it away."

Mulholland Drive was a high rib out of a sea of yellow smog. To Masuto, as always, the sight was unreal and hideous, and his eyes burned. He parked on the edge of a snarl of cars and people that had stopped traffic entirely, and only halfhearted efforts were being made to put the traffic through. As Masuto learned and as he had expected, there were no witnesses. The rescue car was there and two police cars and a sheriff's car and the crawling traffic. And eight motorcycles. The riders were between eighteen and twenty-four years old. They were all bearded and most of them were stripped to the waist. Motorcycle boots, black leather trousers and cigars. They sprawled by their bikes, surly, angry, frustrated. Masuto walked past them to the edge of the slope. The car was about a hundred and fifty yards below, not burnt but thoroughly smashed. Stretcher bearers were crawling carefully up the slope with the woman's body. She was strapped into the stretcher, her face covered, so apparently she was dead. Some cops were around the car.

Lieutenant Pete Bones of the Los Angeles police saw Masuto and called to him, "Howdy, Masao. I thought you had your own stiffs to bury."

"When death comes to town, he stays for a while, doesn't he?"

"That's nicely put. What are you doing up here?"

"Who are the Hell's Angels boys?" pointing to the motorcycle riders.

"They saw the car tumble from around the bend, across that little canyon there."

"Did they see it leave the road?"

Bones shook his head. "They saw one turn and then it come to rest against the rock—the way they tell it."

Masuto nodded thoughtfully, closed his eyes for a long moment, and then nodded again.

"Well, what?" Bones demanded. "It's a Mulholland Drive accident. The books are full of them. If a month went by without someone killing himself on this crazy road, I'd ask for my pension. You live in a crazy town, you get crazy deaths. Look at those bareass lunatics on their damn motorcycles."

"They are more comprehensible and less terrifying than that car down there," Masuto said.

"Why? Furthermore, what does your boss mean, hold it? What should we hold?"

"I didn't want you to drag the car away."

"Without a crane? Furthermore—ah, the hell with it. You want to see the body?"

"Yes. Just to satisfy myself that her skull was caved in from behind—maybe back of the temple."

A cop in plainclothes pulled himself up on the road, and Pete Bones said to him, "Kelly, this here is Masao Masuto from the Beverly force and he has got himself a sort of crystal ball. He says the lady's skull is bashed in from behind."

The man called Kelly gave Masuto a sharp glance and said hello suspiciously.

"Let's go have a look," he told them.

They walked over to where the ambulance man was easing the stretcher into the ambulance.

"How did she die?" Bones asked him.

"Isn't it obvious, officer? You go over Mulholland in one of those tin cans and you die."

"I mean what happened to her physically? And don't be a wiseguy."

"She got banged up. Broken bones, shock, internal injuries, and heart failure."

"What about her skull?"

"Bad fracture."

"How bad?"

"Her skull was smashed in. In nontechnical language, she was struck a hard blow slightly behind her right temple—a very hard blow."

"From the accident?"

"How else?"

"We're asking you!" Kelly snarled. "Don't be such a goddamned wiseguy. How did it happen? Could it happen from the accident?"

"Please uncover her," Masuto asked.

"OK—OK. Don't get excited. You ask me could this skull injury happen from such an accident. Jesus Christ, just look over the edge at that car down there."

He was uncovering the body, when one of the motorcyclists walked over and demanded, "What have you got on us? Every goddamn thing happens in LA County, you got to pin it on us. We want to move on."

"Drop dead," Kelly said.

"Sure. That's the prerogative of fuzz. I answer you back, and you break a pair of brass knucks across my mouth—"

"What the hell is eating this creep?"

"Why don't you just simmer down—" Bones began, but then he and Masuto noticed that the boy's eyes were fixed on the face of the dead woman.

"You know her, buster?" Bones asked him.

"I know nothing. I don't even know my right name. I don't even know how I got here."

"Now just a minute, young feller," Masuto said. "This is not my own place. I'm here as a guest of these officers. But I think they will go along with me if I put my oar in." He glanced at Bones and Kelly who nodded slightly, and Masuto went on, "On the one hand—treat us as people, we treat you as people. I don't really care if you tour the country in a jock—until you break some law. I don't know of any law you broke. Be decent and you ride away from here in ten minutes, because I'll put myself on record for you. But if you make it hard for them, they'll make it hard for you. Is that all right?" he asked Kelly, who nodded without answering.

"What do you want?" the bearded boy asked.

"Who is she?"

"So I know her—so ten thousand guys knew her. She's an old stripper called Peggy Groton. I guess she's almost forty years old. Ran out of steam. She became a hooker, but what's the percentage for an old hooker in this town? You go down on the strip and bend a finger and the chickies come running. Who needs to pay? That's all I know about her. I caught her act, it was lousy. Then I been to parties where she performed and after that for a couple of bucks she would make it. She turns my stomach— lousy whore."

"Sure, she turns your stomach," Bones said.

"I'd like to turn your stomach," Kelly said. "I sure could turn your stomach."

"You said you'd let us go if I cooperated."

"Who the hell wants you?" Bones asked with disgust.

"Is she a user?" Masuto asked.

"How do I know?"

"She's a user," the ambulance man replied. "Or was. You always lose your tenses with these stiffs. Look." He raised her arm, pointed to a cluster of punctures. "She was a big one—user and loser. They all are—all alike."

"But you didn't know she had a habit?" Kelly said to the bearded kid.

"How should I know?"

"Let him go," Masuto said tiredly. "Let the lot of them go. They are unreal. They play a game with you. They irritate you. They take our eyes away from the target."

"Let them go. You tell me, I jump to it," Kelly scowled.

"Oh, hell, let them go," Bones said. "If Masao says they are clear of this, they're clear of it. Send them away. They make me itch and want to scratch just to look at them."

Kelly went to tell them to move on, and Bones said to Masao, "Enough?"

Masuto was looking at a drawn, tired, ravaged face that might once have been lovely. Once. Even in death, Peggy Groton was robbed of identity, of meaning. He shivered.

"Yes, you can take her away."

They bundled the stretcher unceremoniously into the ambulance and drove off. Then the motorcycles roared by, the riders leaving a string of Anglo-Saxon words behind them. One of the rescue men came up the slope with Peggy Groton's purse and handed it to Bones.

"Want to have a look?" Bones asked Masuto.

"There should be about five hundred dollars in there. There might also be the murderer's address and phone number. Maybe. Maybe not. You know, Pete, this monster we are contending with has made every error, every stupid play that a killer can make—and still we can't pin it or stop it."

"And you say there's a half a grand in here—right here in the bag of a broken down hooker."

"Maybe. Maybe not."

"X-ray eyes," said Kelly. "You going to tell us she was murdered?"

"She was."

"How? Who?"

"I'll tell you how—"

Bones had meanwhile opened the purse, and now he was holding out a stack of twenty dollar bills.

"—probably with a lug wrench that the murderer lifted from a filling station. Then, I guess, he threw it down in the yucca there." Masuto bent, picked up a rock, and flung it down the slope. It landed a long way down, far beyond the car. "Somewhere around there—"

"And the money?"

"She was paid off, God help her."

"Six hundred dollars," Bones said.

"She was good," Masuto said thoughtfully.

"How do you know?"

"Names—addresses?"

Bones held up a worn address book. "Do you want to go through it?"

Masuto shrugged. "When you're through with it, I'd appreciate a list of the contents. You might send it up to City Hall."

"Don't you want to see it?"

Masuto shook his head.

"You mean because it's our murder?" Kelly demanded hotly.

"Who said it's murder?" Bones reminded him. "Ain't we got enough problems?"

"He says so. He says the name of the killer is in that book."

"No, I didn't say that at all," Masuto objected. "Still—"

He reached for the little book, riffled through it, saw nothing to catch his eye and then gave it back to Bones. He walked over to his car, and Bones called after him,

"Be in touch!"

"I will," Masuto promised.

The day was wearing through. Masao Masuto had that feeling—not extraordinary for a Buddhist—that the day was a repeat. It had all happened before. It had happened a thousand times before; perhaps nothing changed, perhaps a little changed. He was a stranger in a strange place. He drove east on Mulholland Drive to its connection with Laurel Canyon Boulevard, past the housing developments on top of the skinny ridge of hill. On the Valley side the smog was yellow and noxious; on the other side, on his right, the buttocks of the lower hills were gashed and sheared for the ninety-thousand-dollar homes, where you could sleep above the smog. It occurred to him idly, but with certainty, that he had once known another existence, lived and perished. This was his purgatory. He smiled rather sadly at the thought, remembered the face of Peggy Groton, hooker and onetime stripper, and then turned right onto Laurel Canyon Boulevard. His mind was open and receptive. When he reached Hollywood Boulevard he knew what to do, and he turned east and then south on La Brea.

The bungalow on Sixth Street was even more forlorn revisited than it had been on first sight. In itself—its form, shape, its single tired palm tree in the postage stamp front yard—in itself it was all the brief history, the tawdry illusion that was Hollywood. Just as its mistress was the past of Hollywood, the single long generation that had turned some bright-eyed young girl into this slatternly rooming-house keeper.

She must have been sitting by the window and waiting, for she opened the door, smiled slightly and said, "I knew you'd come back, Mr. Moto."

"How did you know?"

"Horoscopes and stuff. Anyway, I like you. I had dreams about you. That brought you back. What shall I call you? I can't keep on being a crumby racist and calling you Mr. Chan and Mr. Moto. It makes me ashamed of myself.''

"Call me Masao."

"All right, Masao. Will you join me in a cup of tea?" She was quite serious. She was dressed now; her hair was combed; and Masuto liked her better than ever. He did not seek for reasons why. He allowed himself to like her because he liked her.

"I would be honored," he said, bowing slightly. "May I revert to poor politeness? I would find nothing more refreshing than a cup of tea."

She led him into her kitchen, and he was pleased by its cleanliness, by the fact of a modern refrigerator, a good electric stove, and new vinyl floor. Obviously, the kitchen was all that she retained as her home. She brewed tea and sliced up a grocery store poundcake. But she did not offer him a drink of liquor or take one herself.

"I want you to know that I got an attitude toward cops," she said. "I don't like cops. I think that's a healthy attitude, but that's from my point of view."

"I understand. Why do you exclude me?"

"I don't know. Maybe because you don't seem to be a part of this lousy establishment. That's a nice word. When I was a kid, that word didn't exist for us. But it says something. Don't you agree?"

"It says something."

"And you figure you'll come back here and start talking to me and maybe jog my memory and I'll remember about Samantha."

"Possibly."

"What do you want her for, Masao? When they put a high-class educated Beverly Hills cop like you on something, and you keep asking questions, then it must be pretty big. Does it connect up with Mike Tulley's murder?"

He watched her without answering.

"It's been on the radio. Look, sonny, everyone knows, but how you work that poor kid into it is more than I can take. Is the tea all right?"

"Fine."

"No sugar?"

"No."

"You know, I read a lot," she said.

"That's a habit an actress gets into. To wait and wait, to be destroyed and frustrated endlessly—"

"How did you know I was an actress, Masao?"

"That's not such a brilliant guess in Hollywood, is it?"

"There are old bums in Hollywood who aren't actresses."

"You're not an old bum," he said sharply. "Don't lower yourself. Don't denigrate yourself."

"Then don't play games with me, Masao."

"You think I come here and taste your tea to play games with you? If you think that, then you are most mistaken."

She regarded him thoughtfully and silently for a while, and during that time, he sipped his tea and said nothing. Then she tasted her own tea, and asked him, "You're not a Christian, are you?"

"No. I'm a Buddhist."

"That's different, isn't it?"

"Yes, quite different."

"How?"

He shook his head and smiled.

"That's no answer."

"How can I answer you?" he asked seriously.

"You can try."

Masuto held out his hand above the table, the fingers spread. "To you, Mrs. Dolly Baker," he said softly, "skin is something that separates a human hand, a human being from the rest of the universe. Is that so?"

She nodded.

"As I think, the skin connects me with the rest of the universe. Do you understand?"

For almost a full minute, she sat in silence; and then she said to him, "I told you before that I read a lot. You pick up odds and ends of things."

"Whar sort of things?"

"Like the expression the British have for it. They call it a 'copper's nark.' That's good. It sounds like what it is. What do we call it? A fink? A stoolie?"

"I must know about Samantha. Human lives depend on that. Can you say that you will let anyone go to his death if you have the power to change it? Can you sit in judgement? Can you exercise the power of life and death?"

Tears welled into her eyes. Her cheeks became puffy. Suddenly her moment of competence was over and she became a fat, frightened old lady.

"You knew the name all the time," he said.

She nodded.

"Do you want to tell me."

"Her name was Gertrude Bestner, poor kid. God help her. God help her whatever she's into. She was such a loser—"

He walked into the Chief's office, and Kelly and Bones were there, the three of them angry; the Chief annoyed angry, Bones puzzled angry, and Kelly burning angry. Kelly did not like him; Kelly did not like the way he carried himself. Masuto could put himself in Kelly's place. Kelly would tolerate a Nisei, but there are limits to toleration. Kelly and Bones were in Beverly Hills now, and they did not like Beverly Hills or its pocket-size police force. That was understandable.

"You got explaining to do, Masao," the Chief said.

"We all have. That is a condition of mankind."

"Screw the philosophy," said Kelly. "We found the lug wrench."

"The what?"

Bones was the least angry of the three, the most intrigued, the most puzzled. "You remember, Masao, you said that she was murdered with a lug wrench. Then you tossed that rock down into the canyon. Well, we put everyone we had down there and combed out the place. We killed two rattlers—can you imagine?"

"I seen one on Mulholland a week ago," Kelly said. "The hell with that! I want to know how come he knew this broad was knocked over with a lug wrench."

"You got explaining to do, Masao," the Chief repeated seriously.

"I didn't know it," Masuto said. "I guessed."

Kelly threw a flat hand at him and said, "Sure, you guessed. First you guessed she was scragged. Then you guessed the lug wrench. Then you guessed the money in her purse. Balls! That's just too goddamn much guessing for me, and you know what I think about your guesses? I think they're phony as you are!"

"Wait a minute—hold on!" the Chief snapped. "You're in my house now, Kelly. Don't dirty my floors."

"To hell with whose house I'm in! I'm talking about murder—murder that took place in the City of Los Angeles. We got a corpus and we got a murder weapon, and we got enough blood and hair on the lug wrench to link them together. So don't tell me about spitting on the floor. Just tell me where your cop fits in."

Face white, the Chief rose up behind his desk and said very softly, in a voice that Masuto and every other cop on the force had learned to dread, "Just who the hell do you think you're talking to, Kelly! Let me tell you something. I try to be a good neighbor, but one more yap out of you that anyone here is trying to bunco you, and so help me God, I'll lock you up. Make trouble for me you may, but right now you're in Beverly Hills and just keep that in mind."

Kelly was as white as the Chief, and watching them, Masuto felt calm and detached. He himself had been forgotten; they were two men making a power play, and what they felt was their honor had been irritated, scraped bare. Now Bones stepped over to Kelly and took his arm and said, "Just work easy." And then he said to the Chief, "So Kelly's got a big temper and a big mouth. I been his partner six years, Chief. He's a good cop, I am,

Masao is. I don't know what we're ripping at each other for.''

"Forget it," the Chief growled. "What have you got to say for yourself, Masao?"

"Nothing explains intuition," Masuto said. "Shall I try to turn it into reason?"

"Try," the Chief said drily.

"Murder explodes, a sort of chain reaction. We make it too difficult to be a human being, and then something snaps and the person is no longer a person but a killer, and this thing keeps snapping and the killer kills. We are filled with horror, because we inhabit the same unreasonable world—and how long can we remain human? The killer has ceased to be human, and I fit myself into the killer's world. Now I will try to see with his eyes, feel with his nerves, and move as he moves. So everything becomes something else. A car goes over the shoulder on Mulholland Drive. I see it with the eyes of the killer and it becomes a part of the logic of the killer and his progress through our world—"

"But cars go over Mulholland," Bones objected. "It happens every day."

"Then I could be wrong. But what are the odds at this moment? At exactly this moment? I could be wrong, but the odds are that I am right."

"And the lug wrench?"

It was lying on a sheet of paper on the Chief's desk, a garage tool, three-quarters at one end and half an inch at the other, about a foot long and roughly straight.

"You can pick one up in a garage. The attendant turns his back and you're armed. How many things like that are lying around? It could have been a monkey wrench, but the odds are on this. And the money is no mystery either. She had to be paid off in advance."

"Then why didn't the killer take back his roll?"

"No time, maybe. The killer could hear the kids on their motorbikes. Or maybe the money didn't mean enough for the killer to try."

"Six yards and you toss it away like confetti!" Kelly snorted.

"Why was she killed?" the Chief asked.

"The payoff was one thing, but the killer couldn't take any chances."

"OK, Masao—who killed her?" the Chief asked.

"I don't know."

"Why don't you guess," Kelly said.

"Tomorrow I'll guess," Masuto told him.

"But you know," the Chief insisted.

"I don't know."

"Masao, if you're playing games with me—"

"I told you I don't know."

"But you tie this in with Greenberg and Tulley?"

"Both of them. They were both murdered by the same person." He hesitated, and the Chief caught it and said, "It was three, before the car went over."

"All right—you want me out on a limb, I'll go there. His name was Fred Saxton. He was forty-nine years old and he was production manager for Al Greenberg. He was murdered out at the Wide World studios seven weeks ago."

"I know the case," Bones said. "That was an accident. A counterweight came loose and hit him."

"It wasn't an accident," Masuto said.

"How the hell do you know?" Kelly demanded. "We don't have a police force in LA—we just got a bunch of bums, bums who sit around on their asses all day and do nothing. We don't bother investigating a case. No, sir. A guy gets his head broken with a sandbag, we don't give it a second thought. It never occurs to us that maybe someone scrags him. We just write it down as an accident. That's because we're stupid."

"Who's bugging you?" Bones demanded. "Every accident is an accident only until you know better."

"But this joker knows better than anyone."

"It happens."

"The hell it happens," Kelly said. "I'm not satisfied—

not one bit. And speaking for myself, you haven't heard the end of this—not by a long shot."

He went to the desk and began to wrap the lug wrench in the piece of paper.

"Fingerprints?" Masuto asked innocently.

"Fingerprints? You been reading too much Fu Manchu."

He put the lug wrench in his pocket and stamped out. Bones stood looking after him hopelessly, and the Chief sat behind his desk, staring moodily at Masuto.

"Do me a favor, would you, Pete?" Masuto asked Bones.

Bones looked at the Chief, then at Masuto, and said, "You know, Masao, you could do me a favor. What do I do about this? A car goes over the shoulder on Mulholland Drive, and I got to come back to the boss with Kelly riding me and tell him how it's a murder, but we can't tell him who did the murder because you won't guess no more."

"Tomorrow."

"And suppose tomorrow you don't want to guess?"

"Masao," the Chief said, "is this the only way you can play it?"

"I have three of them. One is the killer. They all spin threads, like damned little spiders. Three killers, three motives, three possibilities. I think I could guess. Then I guess wrong, and I have done precisely what the killer desires. This killer is not smart—diabolical but not smart. Every mistake in the book. Blunder after blunder, but because we are dealing with a lunatic, even the blunders work."

"Bones, do him his goddamn favor," the Chief said. "And as for you, Masao—you haven't even filed a report."

"When do I write it? In my sleep?"

"What do you want, Masao?" Bones asked him.

"I want to find out what happened to a kid called Samantha Adams. That's her stage name. Her real name is Gertrude Bestner. She was born in 1936 or 1937, and her last known address was here in Los Angeles on Sixth near

Gower. I'll give you all the facts and details. The last fix I have on her is 1955, a rooming house on Sixth, run then and now by Mrs. Dolly Baker. So you start with 1955 and bring it up to today or as far as it goes. Where is she? Dead or alive? Doing what? Where was she?''

"You don't want much, do you?''

"I want it tonight.''

"You're nuts,'' Bones said.

"Well, then how soon? Shave the hours, and maybe you give a life to someone.''

"Will you back him up, Chief?'' Bones asked.

The Chief nodded.

"Tomorrow. Maybe,'' Bones said. "But only if she stayed in LA. If she took off, maybe a month, a year—or you can kiss your whole project goodby.''

"Try?''

"I said I'd try.''

"I want it the first moment you have it. I'll keep my band open in the car. The moment you have it, you can phone here, and the dispatcher will give it to me.''

"All right. And what do we do with the Peggy Groton thing? Keep it open?''

"You damn well do. It's murder, isn't it?''

"That's what you say, Masao.''

"Tomorrow night I'll buy you both a drink.''

"Saki—and take me out for one of your Japanese meals.''

"If I can fix it with my wife.''

"I thought you Japanese—''

"I am a Nisei,'' Masuto explained.

CHAPTER FIVE

Phoebe Greenberg

On his way out, the girl at the dispatch desk called after him, "Masao!"

He came back, and she told him that there was a call for him. "A Mrs. Greenberg."

It took him a moment to relate it to a face and a person, and then he took the phone, and a low and pleasant voice said, "Sergeant Masuto, this is Mrs. Greenberg—Phoebe Greenberg. Rabbi Gitlin told me you spoke with him this morning."

"Oh, yes—yes, we had a talk."

"He was impressed with you."

"I was impressed with him," Masuto said.

"He said that you were a friend of my—of my husband."

"Yes, in a way."

"In any way—then I would like you to come to the funeral tomorrow. But that isn't what I called you about. I would like to speak to you, if I might."

"When?"

"Now. Is that possible?"

"In ten minutes—or less. I am leaving now."

But the Chief intercepted him and said, "What about it, Masao? You're way out on a limb and I'm with you."

"I told you, tomorrow."

"I sure as God hope so, Masao."

Even with the interruption, Masuto was at the Greenberg

home in eight minutes, and now it was a little after four o'clock in the afternoon. The driveway was full and there were cars in front of the house; and in the living room, Murphy Anderson and his plump wife, Stacy, Jack Cotter alone, and Sidney Burke alone.

They would be off to the chapel later to pay their respects to the deceased. Now they were here to pay their respects to the living.

"Two chapels," Sidney Burke said pointedly. He resented the fact that they were on opposite sides of Beverly Hills, as if he could see no reason on earth why two people in dying should not have the thoughtfulness to be of the same faith.

"Where is Mrs. Greenberg?" Masuto asked.

They explained that she was in the viewing room with Rabbi Gitlin. "I suppose he's some comfort to her," Jack Cotter said, "but the last thing in the world I would have imagined is that Phoebe needed that kind of thing."

"Why?"

"Her relationship with Al—"

"Oh, why don't you shut up, Jack," Anderson interrupted.

"I don't like to be talked to like that," Cotter said coldly.

Stacy Anderson burst out, "Have you met Rabbi Gitlin, Sergeant Masuto? He's absolutely fascinating. He's—"

Rising, Murphy Anderson said, "I think we must go, Stacy, if we want to get to both chapels tonight."

"Poor Lenore," Stacy said, as if she only now remembered that Mike Tulley was dead. "What a dreadful thing she went through. Just imagine—to be trapped on one side of a door while your husband is being murdered by some dreadful woman on the other side of the door. It's perfectly dreadful. Dreadful." She enjoyed the word.

"Sergeant Masuto," Anderson said, "the three of us—Mr. Cotter, Mr. Burke and myself—would like to talk to you tonight. We feel that it's very important."

"Where?"

"My house. I'm on North Rodeo. Say about nine?"

"I'll be there," Masuto agreed.

The Japanese houseman came back into the room at that point and speaking in Japanese told Masuto that Mrs. Greenberg would like to see him.

"Why in hell doesn't he talk English?" Cotter growled.

"I am sorry," Masuto apologized. "He apparently forgot himself with me—there is a natural desire to use one's own language. He simply told me that Mrs. Greenberg would like to see me."

Masuto followed the houseman into the viewing room. Pale, deep circles under her eyes, Phoebe Greenberg greeted him with evident relief. Rabbi Gitlin, sprawled in a chair at one side of the room, nodded at him. Phoebe asked him whether he would have a drink. She had a drink in her hand. She wore a pale green at-home that was most becoming and gave her a sort of ethereal appearance.

"If you wonder why I don't wear black, Mr. Masuto," she said, "it is because my husband hated symbols as a substitute for reality. He bought me this dress himself. I have very few abilities and very few ways to pay tribute to him."

"You have the only ability that counts," Masuto answered.

"And what is that?"

"To see yourself as a human being."

"I don't really understand that," she said, frowning. "But I am glad that you came here. I was very troubled about what I should do, and Rabbi Gitlin suggested that I talk to you. He said that you would hear whatever I had to say with understanding."

"That's very kind of you," Masuto told the rabbi.

Gitlin rose and said, "Perhaps it would be best if I left you alone—both of you."

"No, no," Phoebe protested. "I want you to remain."

"All right." Gitlin sank back into the chair. Masuto

remained standing and Phoebe Greenberg paced nervously as she spoke.

"I didn't want to bring this whole thing up. I wasn't going to. My husband was a very sick man, Mr. Masuto. I knew this, because his physician told me and also instructed me in what to do in an emergency. I can't talk very well about the relationship between my husband and me. We were only married three years, and his illness precluded any normal relationship. But I think I worshipped the ground he walked on. I never looked at another man after I married him, Mr. Masuto. Well, that's done, and I cannot weep or carry on. Some can, some can't. I was going to wash this whole wretched thing out of my mind until Mike was killed today. Tell me, do you think that the same person who murdered Mike Tulley killed my husband?"

"Let me answer that obliquely, Mrs. Greenberg. No one will ever know, unless there is some sort of a confession, whether or not your husband was murdered. But I do know this—that if he was murdered, it was the same person. And I can tell you that this same person coldbloodedly killed two others."

"Oh no! Who?"

"Did you know a man called Fred Saxton?"

"Yes—yes, I knew Fred. He worked for Al—for my husband. But his death—it was one of those awful accidents."

"I don't think so, any more than the death of a woman called Peggy Groton, whose car went over the shoulder up on Mulholland Drive today, was an accident. There is very little doubt in my mind that both of these people were murdered."

"That's a pretty terrifying statement," Gitlin said. "What are you trying to tell us, Sergeant? That four murders were committed? Then what kind of horror is loose among us?"

"You're asking for a philosophical conclusion, rabbi. I am only a policeman."

"It's not fashionable to faint, is it?" Phoebe asked.

Masuto and the rabbi helped her to a chair. Very pale, she sat there and said, "When I was a little girl, my mother used to tell me about fainting and smelling salts and that sort of thing. It was very fashionable once, but I guess no one faints any more. You never hear about it. I don't even have smelling salts in the house, whatever they are." She took a deep breath and went on, "I am going to tell you about this, Mr. Masuto. It may be wrong and vile to speak about it, because it happened a long time ago. But I must tell you about it—I must."

Masuto waited. The rabbi glanced from Phoebe to Masuto, opened his mouth to say something, then clamped it shut.

"A terrible thing happened eleven years ago on a set where my husband was producing a TV segment. A man— well, it was Sidney Burke, because I will have to name names or this whole thing is meaningless. Sidney got some young kid actress to agree to have sex with some men on the set in return for a tiny part in the show. You have to be an actress yourself to know what these crazy kids will do for a part—any part. They all live with some kind of childish, pathetic dream that once they are seen, they will all instantaneously become Natalie Wood. So Sidney arranged this ghastly affair and—oh, it's so hard for me to speak about it."

"I know about it," Masuto said shortly.

"You do?" She was genuinely surprised.

"Who told you about this? Your husband?"

She nodded.

"What did he tell you was his role in the affair?"

She stared at Masuto for a long moment, and then she shook her head. "No. Oh, no. You are not going to tell me that he lied to me—"

"I didn't say he lied to you. I only asked you to tell me what he said was his role in the affair."

She turned desperately to Rabbi Gitlin, who said, "Tell

him, Phoebe. Let's get this whole filthy business out into the open. There's no other way.''

Then she said deliberately, ''My husband did not lie to me, Mr. Masuto. He told me that the moment he found out what was happening, he put an end to it. He was sick and angry.''

''I don't think he lied,'' Masuto said. ''That's essentially the same thing that Murphy Anderson told me—that he came on it and put a stop to it.''

''Thank you,'' she whispered.

''Still, it is very important that you tell me exactly what your husband told you about this affair—and anything else you ever heard about it.''

''But if what my husband told me was true, why was he murdered? She must have known—''

''Who must have known, Mrs. Greenberg?''

''Samantha.''

''Oh?''

''I said Samantha. Do you know who she is?'' she cried.

''As much as anyone knows who she is.''

''Then why—''

''That will not help,'' Masuto said. ''You are piling up premises. You are trying to be logical. But most of the logic we live with is a lie, and most of our attempts to be logical are only attempts to evade the reality. So if we have a puzzle, stop trying to solve it. Don't cling to thoughts and notions. Let them pass through your mind and then dismiss them—or treat them all with equal indifference. Nothing that will ever happen or become known to you can change anything about your husband's relationship to you.''

She turned to the rabbi pathetically. ''Is that true?''

''Quite true,'' Gitlin said.

''But if you will answer my questions, *you* can help,'' Masuto told her.

''What questions?''

"As far as you know, who were the men involved in this incident eleven years ago?"

"Must I?"

"I know their names," Masuto said. "I am asking for corroboration, which is very important."

She took a deep breath and nodded. "Very well. You know about Mike Tulley. Poor Mike. He walked into all these things. He always had to prove that he was a man, and that bitch he was married to never let him believe he was a man for more than five minutes. Oh, I am sorry over poor, silly Mike. Then Jack Cotter." She made a face.

"How can you explain about Cotter? Jack is a Hollywood cowboy. Maybe the only time he was actually alive was when he put on his cowboy suit and his six-guns on the back lot. It's a special spongy kind of brain. They really think they are cowboys. The back lot is the universe. It's real. Do I make any sense?"

"You make sense," Masuto said. "And Murphy Anderson?"

"Murphy. I could never understand it about Murphy, but then I appear to understand very little about men. Sidney Burke, of course. What can one say about Sidney? Max Green—poor Max. He was such a fool—poor Max died of a heart attack a year ago, and then Freddy Saxton. Of course. That's why you asked me about him. And it wasn't an accident?"

"I am afraid not," Masuto said.

"What kind of a devil is she? Freddy has six children. Six kids. So he did something vile eleven years ago. Does that condemn him to death and his six kids—what does this all mean?"

Masuto turned to the rabbi, who shook his head. "I am past speculation on that point. I don't know what anything very much means—except that we store up horror. We prepay for it, so to speak, and then we are astonished when it happens."

"What can one say about Sidney Burke?" Masuto asked her.

"What? Really, what?" She sighed. "When I asked Al why he didn't break Sidney's back, he said a very peculiar thing—that you cannot make a moral judgement of a person who is utterly without morality. Anyway, Sidney is Hollywood—I mean the place is full of Sidneys. Sidney doesn't do evil—he is just completely unaware of any difference between good and evil. Sidney is the ultimate amoral. If you asked him about that wretched gangshag he set up eleven years ago, he might be nervous—but not ashamed. He was doing everyone a favor. He was doing Samantha a favor by getting her a job on TV. He was doing the boys a favor by getting them a free lay on the set. And he was being progressive. He was forwarding the whole industry in his own way. That's the way Sidney is. He comes in dressed in his black silk suit with his pointed shoes and his thirty-dollar white-on-white tab shirt, and he gives you that big grin of his and a big kiss, and he never really gets angry at anything you say to him and he's also thinking of some kind of favor he can do for you. That's because he wants so much to be liked—"

Her voice trailed away. Masuto was listening with astonishment. This was Phoebe Greenberg, who should have been a senseless blonde who never made it as an actress. He looked at the rabbi, who permitted himself a slight smile.

"I go home," Masuto said—"that is, sometimes I go home, and then when I do my wife says to me, tell me about today. What kind of a day was it?"

"It might surprise you," the rabbi said, "to find that her day is equally inscrutable."

"Perhaps. But we have been talking about this and that, Mrs. Greenberg. You didn't call me over here to chat. You called me here to tell me who is Samantha, didn't you?"

"What a notion!"

"But you did."

"I think you fancy yourself, Mr. Masuto, because you happen to be Japanese. It gives you a sort of racial crystal ball which you can bring out whenever the mood suits you."

"I think we both fancy ourselves," Masuto said flatly. "All people do. All people build their own aura, their own mask that separates them from the world. Perhaps mine is that of the inscrutable Oriental—I imagine the rabbi chose that word deliberately—and Rabbi Gitlin goes through life as a large, confused innocent, as much of a mask as my own Oriental magic kit. And you, Mrs. Greenberg—"

"And me?"

"You are the professional Hollywood dumb blonde. Do you mind me being a bit shaken by what is underneath?"

"And how do you know that I am a professional dumb blonde?" she asked coldly.

"A word here and a word there. I listen. So why don't we stop fencing. Who do you think is Samantha?"

"Shall I tell him?" she asked the rabbi.

"That's up to you, Phoebe."

"Very well. Samantha is Trude Burke, Sidney's wife."

The Japanese butler brought tea and tiny sandwiches, and he told Phoebe that there had been a call from the funeral chapel and that people were beginning to arrive, and that some relatives of Mr. Greenberg were arriving from the East and would go directly there, that his two sons were expected—his daughter was in Europe and could not be reached—and when would she be there?

"I should go now," she said, "but I must talk to Mr. Masuto. Please have some sandwiches, Mr. Masuto."

"I'll go there directly," said Rabbi Gitlin. "I can arrange for my wife to be there."

"The truth is, I am afraid to go there," she said.

"Well, that's natural, Phoebe. Take your time, but come. You must. Meanwhile, my wife and I will constitute ourselves a sort of semifamily committee. There are no other relatives here in Los Angeles, are there?''

"No, but Murph is the closest friend Al had, and he and Stacy will be there. I'll try to come within the hour."

Masuto, his mouth full of sandwich—eating with the feeling that this would be as close to dinner as circumstances might permit—motioned for the rabbi to wait.

"Please." He swallowed quickly.

"What is it, Sergeant?"

"Have you spoken about this, Mrs. Greenberg—about your feeling that Trude Burke is Samantha—to anyone else?"

"No. Only to you and Rabbi Gitlin."

"Good. Now listen to me, Rabbi—you are not to mention this, not even in passing, not even as a nameless suspicion, not to Anderson or Cotter or Burke. And not to their wives—"

"But surely," Phoebe broke in, "you don't—"

"I damn well do, and I tell you, Rabbi, that one word about this can mean Mrs. Greenberg's death. No—one word about it *will* mean Mrs. Greenberg's death."

" 'Damn well,' " the Rabbi repeated. "Slang sits oddly with you, you know. Of course—just as you say."

He left them then, and Masuto stuffed another sandwich into his mouth, worked it down quickly, dialed City Hall, got the Chief and said to him, "I want two cops on motorcycles, one in front of the Greenberg place on North Canon and one in the mews behind it, and I want it covered all night."

"You know that means I got to put two men on overtime," the Chief pointed out.

"With all respect to my esteemed boss," Masuto said, "I am aware of his financial difficulties. My heart bleeds for the poverty of those who guard the wealthiest city in the world."

*   *   *

The Chief's "Go to hell!" was audible across the room.
Masuto turned back to Phoebe to apologize, and she, in
the midst of pouring tea, had stopped and was staring at
him bleakly.

"What have I done!" she said.

"Oh? What have you done, Mrs. Greenberg?"

"You believe what I said about Trude."

"Don't you?" he asked.

"No. No. Of course not! Oh, what a precious Oriental
dunce of a detective you are to believe me."

"Then why did you tell me what you told me?"

"Because I believed it. But I didn't believe it because it
was true. I believed it because I detest her, and because
Rosie Valero, who does my hair, told me that Trude's
gorgeous strawberry blond is a bottle job, and that they do
her once a week, and they not only do her hair but her eye
lashes and her eyebrows and her damned pubic tufts and
whatever other hair she has on her body, and Rosie thinks
she had some sort of nose job. And why should she go to
that kind of trouble for a worm like Sidney unless she was
pretending to be a horse of another color. And the thought
of Al—of poor, fat, good Al, who was so kind to everyone
and who never hurt a soul in his life—the thought of him
being murdered by some rotten little slut, well, it was just
more than I could stand, and so I told you. But I didn't
believe it. I just had to tell you."

"But you told the Rabbi first?"

"Yes."

"And what did he say?"

"He said that he didn't put much stock in it and that he
didn't think you would put much stock in it, so it couldn't
do Trude any harm, but that I should go ahead and tell you
and get myself a good, deep condition of guilt, which
would act as some kind of a psychic purge, and then I
would hate myself, and then I would feel better."

"He's a remarkable man," Masuto answered thoughtfully.

"Yes, indeed. And now you hate yourself."

"I think I hate you, because you are stupid enough to believe me."

"How do you know that I believe you, Mrs. Greenberg?"

"Because you called for those cops to be around the house all night."

"To protect you from a killer. You know, there are a dozen holes in your story, but isn't one thing absolutely obvious?"

"What?"

"That Samantha would have to be diabolically clever, and that the only one of the lot of you clever enough to be her is you—yourself, Mrs. Greenberg."

"How dare you!"

"And that lovely hair of yours—isn't it what you call a bottle job?"

"Oh, what a miserable, wretched—oh no. No. You can't do this, because I am a woman all alone here. Insult me. Accuse me of the murder of my husband."

"Dear Mrs. Greenberg," he sighed. "Have I accused you of anything? I am afraid my deadpan humor is perfectly wretched. I will tell you flatly what you already know—that you are not Samantha and that you are a very clever, and more importantly, a reasonably wise woman. I admire you a great deal. But I think I know people enough to realize that you would weep if you had to kill a mouse."

She nodded silently.

"You know," he added, "Mr. Burke was the only one who knew Samantha before he got her into that dressing room. So he could hardly blunder into a marriage with her."

"I wonder," she said. "I've been beastly, haven't I? Please do have another cup of tea and some sandwiches."

CHAPTER SIX

Sidney Burke

Masuto was surprised to see that Sidney Burke was still in the living room, sitting in a corner silently and listening to one of the friends of the deceased. There were about a dozen people there. Burke was listening and waiting, and when he saw Masuto, he jumped to his feet and intercepted the detective—who already, simply because he was a Nisei—was the object of all the eyes in the room.

"Let's shake this place," he said softly to Masuto. "I got to talk to you."

"I thought you went to the chapel with the others," Masuto said.

"Changed my mind." They were outside now. "I don't have a car here, Sarge. Can we get in yours and drive a little and talk a little? I know a little place up on La Cienega and Sunset, where we can have a quiet corner and I'll buy you a hamburger."

"I'll buy my own hamburger," Masuto said.

"That's an honest cop for you," said Burke. "So I won't corrupt you with a hamburger. Buy your own and I will remember it as the last untarnished hamburger in Hollywood. Can you spare me half an hour? And is the place OK with you?"

"What do you call it?"

"The Quiet Cow."

They got into Masuto's car, and he called the station on

his phone and told the Chief that he was going to a place called The Quiet Cow with Sidney Burke, and would the Chief have the dispatcher call his wife and tell her he would not be home for dinner.

"And I have a meeting with Cotter and Anderson and Burke later at Anderson's house."

"Did you ask for it?" the Chief demanded sourly.

"Anderson asked for it."

They drove off, and Burke said, "Great cops have bigger cops upon their back to bite them, and bigger cops have bigger cops and so ad infinitum."

"That's very good," Masuto admitted. "What can I do for you, Mr. Burke?"

"It ain't original."

"I didn't think so."

"OK. So by now you know about Samantha."

"A little."

"You know more than a little," Burke said. "Everybody's crapping in their pants because each and every one of them thinks he is next on Samantha's little list."

"But you're not worried."

"Worried? Jesus God, would I be riding around with a cop if I was not worried? Of course I am worried. It's the goddamn power complex. Kill one; you know it can be done. With the second, you are riding high; and with the third, she is a lousy little tin god—"

"Who is?"

"Samantha Adams—who else."

"What do you mean—third?"

"Don't put me on, Sarge. You know about Fred Saxton."

"An accident, I am told."

"Then you are told wrong."

"Samantha?"

"Don't kid me, Sarge. Don't put me on. I'm no hero and I don't intend to live the rest of my life with loose bowels. I am tired of being nervous."

They were up on Sunset now, and as they approached

the Strip the traffic stopped, and there was a sound like a thousand kids yelling. A half a dozen deputies came running by, carrying riot batons, and across the avenue, a stream of teenagers, shouting taunts and defiance, poured in among the cars.

"That's the way it is with those long-hair creeps," Burke said. "Never taught them any discipline or morality. That's the way kids are brought up today."

Masuto managed a turn into Larrabee and headed for Wilshire. "That's no place for a Beverly Hills cop," he said. "I know a little Danish place on Wilshire. Will you settle for that?"

"Anyway you say. I got no more appetite anyway, and you can't afford what I consider a place fit to eat in. Just so long as I put it to you."

"Go ahead," Masuto said.

"You're running this case? Correct me if I am wrong."

"I like to think so," Masuto said.

"All right. Now listen—today, only a few hours ago, maybe two o'clock, maybe two-fifteen, I am driving along Mulholland toward Laurel Canyon, and a little red MG zips by me from the opposite direction. I see a strawberry head and I do a double take, and maybe half a mile along, I say to myself, that's got to be Trude, my wife. But I am not sure, because when a hot car passes you on Mulholland, you are watching the road not the car, but it fits her car and her head. Maybe. Next thing I know, I see prowl cars and an ambulance and kids with motorbikes—those lousy creeps with the beards—and I know there's some kind of accident, but the sight of blood makes me ill. I throw up when I see a lot of blood. Not good. So I crawl past, and that's that, except that I do a second double take. I see you. First I see you and I don't think nothing about it, because where there's an accident, there should be cops. Period. Then I say to myself, this part of Mulholland is Los Angeles, so what is a Beverly Hills cop doing casing a job in Los Angeles, when he should be sitting with his head in his hands trying to figure out who knocked over Mike Tulley and Al Goldberg?''

''That's pretty good.''

''Well, it's no Charlie Chan film, but I got cops and murder on my brain, and I get home and there's Trude's MG in the carport, and now I am a nervous type, so I feel the hood. It's hot. So I go into the house and Trude's doing her nails to go to the chapel tonight, and I say to her, 'What were you doing up on Mulholland Drive, baby? I thought you were a big girl and grown out of doing tricks with the MG?' So she says to me, 'Drop dead. I never went near Mulholland Drive.' ''

In the little Danish restaurant, Masuto sipped coffee and munched pastry and regarded Sidney Burke with interest and a degree of wonder. Burke ate little. He tried to explain to Masuto his distaste for a restaurant that was low-priced.

''Regardless of the quality of the food?'' Masuto had asked curiously.

''My drawing is four thousand dollars a week, Sarge,'' Burke said. ''Apart from expenses. What I eat in a restaurant is expenses. I can't explain that to you. It is not simply a matter of screwing the government. I get kicks from that, but that ain't all. I got the biggest and best PR outfit on the Coast. I got a very important interest in Northeastern Films. I got other interests. So I don't eat in a place like this. I can't afford to. Suppose someone says, I seen Burke—see? No good.''

''How about The Quiet Cow?''

''That's a hamburger joint where the hamburgers are three bucks.''

''I can't afford three bucks for a hamburger.''

''I wasn't going to bribe you,'' Burke said. ''I was just going to tell them you're a cop. You don't think Joey Donsen who runs the place is such a schmuck he's going to charge a cop.''

Now, however, Burke was trying to tell Masuto about his wife, and he kept saying that he had to be sincere. "I got to be sincere," he told Masuto, "otherwise I can't make you understand about this girl I'm married to. Not that I got anything against Trude—you understand—she's just a louse. But that doesn't mean that Sidney Burke is a schmuck. I knew she was a louse when I married her. This is a kid, I just had to look at her and I was off. I want to be sincere. I am not the kind of a guy who flips over a tomato. What was worth banging, I banged—"

"But just to come back to the problem that confronts us," Masuto said, "with due deference to your sincerity, how can you believe that your wife is Samantha? You knew Samantha. You brought her to the studio—"

"I knew Samantha? Listen, Sarge, in the past fifteen years, I knew maybe two, three hundred broads who are maybe enough like Samantha to be her sister. The blonde American way of life, with the little round puss, the turned up nose, the blue eyes, and the shapely ass. You can pick out ten any morning at the counter at Schwab's. At Central Casting, they decorate the walls with them. You wave a contract out at Santa Monica Beach, and you got a thousand of them. What do I know about Samantha? I picked her up at the counter at the Beverly Wilshire, paid for her hamburgers, gave her a ride and a night of pleasure. I thought the kid was grateful. She wanted a job more than anything in the world, so I got her a job. The boys would have been nice to her if she had just said two words. What's to get excited about?"

"Did Anderson tell you about the phone call from her?"

"That's right."

"And you think your wife could be Samantha. Isn't that a little farfetched? That she married you for revenge?"

"Farfetched! Sarge, you been spoiled by Japanese girls. This tomato of mine had her revenge in the first thirty days, and I been married to her for two years. I married my first wife when I was twenty-three. We got divorced two years later. She had a lousy disposition, if you know what I mean, the cranky kind. But compared to Trude, she was an angel. Believe me, I am being sincere."

"Still, you must remember Samantha."

"Absolutely. Just take a good look at Trude. She weighs at least ten-fifteen pounds more than Samantha. Samantha was a skinny kid. Samantha had that kind of pale, yellow-white do-it-yourself blond hair. She wore it like a kid, combed down straight. Trude's got a head of strawberry-blond curls that just sit natural all over her head. It must cost her a hundred dollars a week—all over, every place on her body there's a hair, it's dyed. She had a nose job seven years ago, not for looks but for what they call a deviated septum. Would you believe me, she hasn't got one picture from before that nose job—not one."

"That's understandable," Masuto said.

"Understandable? Sarge, on the question of broads, I am maybe an expert—in a small way. Would I want to pin this on my own wife, if I did not have a position? I am trying to be absolutely sincere. It is not understandable. A dame like Trude, she lives by her pictures. She can't always be looking into a mirror, can she?"

"When did you first have a suspicion that your wife might be Samantha?"

"Seven weeks ago—when that sandbag killed Freddie Saxton. One of the grips on the set saw a girl beat it out—just got a glimpse of her, and that was right before he found out about Freddie. The cops over there in the Valley talked to him, but he couldn't describe the girl. He just saw her run past and out of the soundstage, and he caught a glimpse of her."

Masuto filled his cup with coffee again and began to consume another Danish pastry, reflecting on the fact that so much evil is mediocre beyond belief; so much vileness, the writhing of frustrated children trapped in the bodies of adults. Anyway, it was not his to judge. He even felt a little ashamed of himself when he said, "Naturally, Mr. Burke, you brought the grip a picture of your wife."

"That's my duty as a citizen, Sarge."

"Naturally. But the grip could make no identification."

"No."

"Did he remember the girl having red hair?"

"All he could remember was blond. So what? You think Trude's some kind of idiot? She'd wear a wig."

"Does she have wigs?" Masuto asked.

"Sarge, wake up. You're running with the wrong crowd. There ain't a dame in this town doesn't have a closet full of wigs."

Leaving this statement unchallenged, Masuto asked about detective agencies. "Surely, you would have thought of that, Mr. Burke?"

"I did."

"Which agency?"

"Intermountain. They're up on—"

"I know where they are." Masuto nodded. "Who do you deal with there—Frank Gillespie?"

"No, his partner, Adam Meyerwitz. I been dealing with them for years and they can be trusted one hundred percent. So I put them on the job. I told Meyerwitz the whole story. I told him I wanted it quick."

"Just out of curiosity," Masuto said, "what do they charge for a job like that?"

"Six hundred dollars a day. They were on it five days."

Masuto whistled.

"Well, there you are," said Burke. "You don't see them making no heroes out of Beverly Hills cops, do you, Sarge? A private eye, that's something else. He's America's lover boy."

"And what did Intermountain give you for six hundred dollars a day?"

"Nothing. Not one stinking, lousy thing. They found out that Trude Steffenson, the name she had when I married her, was not the name she was born with. But they couldn't come up with the name she was born with. They found indications that she had come to Hollywood in 1952, but from where they don't know, and they can't put a finger on her before 1961. Can you imagine? Can you imagine being married to a broad who's a phony from the word go? When I think of the way that broad took me in—''

"Are they still on it?"

"Are you kidding? At six hundred dollars a day? Anyhow, she's a smartass broad and she felt something, and then she went to the Pinkertons and hired her own man and found out and she comes home and tells me that she'd ruin me forever in the industry if I ever try something like that again.''

"Could she?"

"She could make plenty of trouble for me. That's gratitude, Sarge. I marry a broad like that, who's worth maybe a yard for a night to some jackass from Kansas, and I give her everything in the world, but everything, and what do I get?''

"You know when Mike Tulley was killed?"

"Today."

"I mean the time."

"About twelve-thirty," Burke replied.

"Did you ask your wife where she was at that time?"

"I did," Burke said.

"And what was her answer?"

"Drop dead."

"What?"

"I mean that was her answer, Sarge. That's what you asked me, isn't it? Isn't it?"

"I asked you that."

"So I told you. She says to me, 'Drop dead.' ''

"Nothing else?"

"Nothing else. We don't have conversations these days. Does the butcher talk to the goose he picks out? So why should she talk to me?''

"You haven't tried to divorce her?"

"With what she's got on me?"

"Will she be at the chapel now?"

"Who knows? Murph invited her to his house tonight for the meeting or whatever he intends to do."

"He did?"

"That's right. He did."

"Suppose we drive over to the chapel now," Masuto said. "I don't think Mrs. Greenberg will be offended by my presence there."

The chapel was on Wilshire, about a mile toward downtown. Here Greenberg's body would lie through the night, and from here it would be taken for burial the following day. There would be a brief service at Mt. Ephriam Cemetery the following day, after which the actual burial would take place. Now, at the chapel, close friends and relatives were gathering. Anderson and Cotter would both be there. From there, they and their wives would go to Anderson's house.

As Masuto drove his car into the parking lot behind the chapel, Sidney Burke voiced his uncertainties. "It's not like I don't regard you as a gentleman, Sarge," he said, "but won't it look peculiar?"

"Because I am a cop or because I am a Nisei?"

"Well, you got to admit that the combination is peculiar."

"Yet curiously enough," Masuto said quietly, "I was a friend of Al Greenberg."

"You?"

"Myself," Masuto nodded. "So if you don't mind, I'll pay my respects."

"Mind? Why should I mind?" He led the way toward the chapel. "Mind. You talk like I'm running this show. I don't mind. I'm the last one in the world to mind."

They entered the chapel, where they were met by a man in tails with a professionally funereal countenance. He asked them which of the several rooms in use that evening they were concerned with, and when they specified Al Greenberg, he sighed just enough and guided them to the proper place. There were about fifty people in the room, a high-ceilinged room, decorated in a popular West Coast style known as dubious-Hollywood-Gothic. Masuto entered and stood silently just inside the doorway. Burke joined Anderson and Cotter, and then Cotter walked purposefully over to Masuto and said hoarsely, "You ought to know better than to come here. Is nothing sacred to a cop?"

"I am a Beverly Hills cop, Mr. Cotter," Masuto said without rancor.

"What is that supposed to mean? That there's nothing sacred in Beverly Hills?"

"It's my own poor sense of humor, Mr. Cotter. I know this is neither the time or the place. But I must ask you something."

"You're right when you say this is neither the time nor the place."

"But if you would give me a moment—"

"OK—OK—ask."

"Did Samantha get the bit part she was brought down there for? I mean, was she actually filmed?"

"Big thought!" Cotter said sarcastically. "You really got it pinned."

"Do you mind answering."

"No. Jesus God, man, do you think she was in any condition to act?"

"I wasn't there," Masuto smiled, "so I don't speculate on her condition. Just as I make no judgements about what happened there."

"You could go too far, buddy boy. And you still haven't explained by what process you horn in here tonight."

"I felt I had to talk to Mrs. Greenberg and persuade her to join us tonight," Masuto said patiently.

"She is joining us. So that's that."

"Still, I must explain my presence. She's seen me now. I must explain the misunderstanding."

Cotter shook his head and walked back to join Anderson

and Burke. Phoebe Greenberg, who had seen Masuto now, came over to him and said, "Why did you come here, Sergeant? Has some new terrible thing happened?"

"No. But I must speak to you."

"I'll see you later at Murph Anderson's house. I can't talk here. My husband's family is here. They have no notion that there was anything unusual about his death."

"I must talk to you now. If you would only step out into the corridor with me. I won't take more than five minutes of your time."

"Very well." She sighed, and he held the door open for her and she walked through. Outside, he looked at her sharply, and then said, "No one will ask you whether you loved your husband. Did you?"

"I loved him very much," she said flatly. "He saved my life. He gave me back to life. He was one of the few good men I have ever known. He did everything for me, and I did very little for him. Does that answer your question, Mr. Masuto?"

"Yes. Will you do something for him now?"

"What can I do for him? He's dead."

"Help me to take his murderer."

"He was murdered?"

"Yes. I have no doubt about it."

"How?"

"I think the murderer held a cushion over his face. He had an attack and died."

"What do you want me to do?"

"I want you to be at World Wide Studios tomorrow at ten-thirty or so in the morning. Do you have anything filming now?"

"Yes, we have two pilots in work. But you don't understand. The funeral is tomorrow."

"I do understand. Then you have makeup people there. I don't want you to make any arrangements in advance. Just turn up and tell them to make you up immediately."

"Who? Mr. Masuto, you simply do not have the faintest

notion of how a studio operates. I can't just walk on to a soundstage and tell the makeup people to go to work on me. You have a film in process. You have a production manager, a director, a cast—''

''I know all that,'' Masuto said impatiently. ''Aren't you forgetting one thing?''

''What's that?''

''That you own Northeastern Films.''

''I do not. The partners will buy my husband's shares.''

''Next week, next month. At this moment, you are the widow of the president. No one will question anything you ask—just so long as you make it plain that you are the boss. Believe me.''

''Even a crazy request like makeup—?''

''Yes. Any request.''

''And what shall I make up as?'' she asked hopelessly.

''A middle-aged woman. Dark wig. Glasses. Padding around your middle.''

''And that will help catch the murderer?''

''Yes.''

''You give me your word?''

''Yes—except that all plans have a point of failure. This is dangerous, very dangerous. I will protect you as much as one human being can protect another. But it will still be very dangerous.''

''And if I refuse, Mr. Masuto?''

''Then it will be even more dangerous, because the killer will kill you. We will try to protect you, but for how long?''

''I will do it,'' she said matter-of-factly.

''Good. You get into costume. Do you know where Stage 6 is?''

''The stage where poor Freddie died?''

''That's right. At exactly 11:10, I will be outside of Stage 6. I will look for you. If you don't see me, walk on and then return. But under no circumstances must you enter Stage 6 without me.''

"Suppose I don't see you at all?"

"Then go back to where your people are shooting and call the Beverly Hills police and find out what happened to me, or whether there is any message for you."

"All right."

"And tonight, not one word of this. Not to anyone. Not to Anderson and not to his wife. Not to the Rabbi. Do you understand me?"

"I understand you, Mr. Masuto."

"Good. You are a very brave woman. Will you tell Mr. Burke to go with the others. I am going to leave now."

She nodded and returned to the mourning room. Masuto left the chapel and walked around to the parking lot. He got into his car, started the motor and drove slowly past the chapel into Wilshire Boulevard. Out of the corner of his eye, he saw that a side door into the chapel was half open. Behind the door, only darkness, and then as he came close to it, the darkness was broken by a tiny tongue of light, almost like the flicker of a firefly. There must have been a silencer on the gun—or perhaps the slight whip of a twenty-two caliber pistol was absorbed into the sound of his own motor.

It was when he stopped his car out on Wilshire and looked at the small, neat hole in his windshield that he realized the gun was a twenty-two, probably one of those tiny, deadly little pistols that nestle so well in a lady's handbag.

He leaped out of the car and ran back into the chapel, stumbling and skinning his knuckles in the stygian blackness of the side door. He crouched there, licking at his hand and cursing himself for a fool. What had he expected to find? If the murderer had waited, he, Masuto, would now be dead. Nothing put down Masuto so completely as to discover a wide, foolish hole in his own intelligence.

CHAPTER SEVEN

Stacy Anderson

Masuto took a liberty that his chief would certainly note and resent and called his wife on his car radiophone. The children were asleep, and she was reading a mystery novel by Rex Stout. She was rather nervous, and pleased that he had called her; and after telling him about the children, she suggested that it would be a nice thing some day to take a vacation and go to New York City.

"A very long and expensive trip."

"In this book, it is a very pleasant place. Perhaps you will stop being a policeman and earn a great deal of money."

"That's not likely," he said.

"Will I ever see you again?"

"I think it's possible," he said.

"Now you tease me."

"Never."

"You have no more use for me, your wife, but only for the beautiful blondes one sees in Hollywood."

"That's right."

"I know. I know. There was a picture of Mike Tulley's wife in the evening paper—in the *Times*. She is so beautiful."

"The *Times* is a morning paper."

"Don't we get it in the evening? Is she as good as she is beautiful?"

"Who?"

"Lenore Tulley."

"I am happy to speak to you, and I love you very much," he said.

"But you never tell me about the wonderful things that happen to you."

"I love you anyway," he said.

"Michael has a sore throat."

"Is it bad?"

"No. I gave him some aspirin. I am sure he'll be better tomorrow."

Then Masuto said his goodbys, put away the telephone, and fingered the tiny hole in his windshield. He felt better since speaking to his wife. He felt better able to face the rest of the night.

Murphy Anderson's house on Rodeo Drive was a gigantic Beverly Hills-half-timber-Tudor. Stacy Anderson must have left the chapel soon after Masuto, since she was already home to open the door for him and usher him into a red leather, brass nail, Oriental rug interior and through the baronial hall into an immense sunken living room, which sported medieval banners from its cross-beams. In a fireplace large enough to drive a sport car through, two huge imitation logs glowed with light and warmth, and in one corner a suit of armor leaned moodily on its spear.

"I felt someone had to be here to welcome you, Inspector," Stacy Anderson said, "so I made my apologies and rushed home."

"Sergeant, Mrs. Anderson."

"Sergeant?"

"I mean, we don't have inspectors. We should, I often feel."

"You are humorous. I mean, for a Japanese. We never give Orientals any credit for a sense of humor, and I fear we make a dreadful mistake—don't you?"

"I really couldn't say, Mrs. Anderson. I have never been in the Orient."

"What a shame!"

Could she be as stupid as she appeared, Masuto wondered, as insensitive and gauche? Or was she putting him on? Was she possibly one of those extraordinary women who can move through life playing the role of the fool, and who wears a fool's mask to cover the intelligence? Now it was hard to say, and he rejected any quick judgements. Certainly, she was a beautiful and seductive woman, about thirty-one or thirty-two, round, just the slightest bit plump, pale blue eyes contrasting strangely with her black hair. For the chapel, she had put on a dress of black velvet—a stunning repeat for her glowing hair. Masuto reflected that in today's America, it is almost unthinkable that a blond woman should dye her hair black. Blondness was big business, a passion, a semiracist ingredient of the mythology current in the land. Yet few women could adorn themselves with anything more beautiful than Stacy Anderson's hair. Why shouldn't she dye it black?

He became conscious of the fact that he was staring at her and pulled his gaze away. She was in no way disturbed. Quite to the contrary, she was pleased at being the object of his admiration. Masuto had the very strong feeling that she would be pleased to be the object of any man's admiration, and he was in no position to draw conclusions. Why Murphy Anderson had married her was only too evident, and why she had married him was almost equally obvious.

"Isn't this a huge room?" she asked. "You know, Murph has two children from his first marriage and they spend their summers with us and they're absolutely divine youngsters, so when Murph and I decided to buy a place here in Beverly Hills, I felt we should have something that was both homey and big enough for the kids to romp around in. This seemed just to fill the bill perfectly, and there's a wonderful big pool and a tennis court out back. But do you know, Inspector—''

"Sergeant," Masuto said.

"Of course. Sergeant. You know, they always seem to be a little overawed by the house until they get the hang of it. That takes time, you know.''

"I suppose so."

"Do you like my dress?"

"It's very attractive.''

"Thank you, dear Inspector. I wonder whether you would suggest something I might serve. I thought of champagne, but this isn't that kind of a party, is it?"

"I'm afraid not.''

"Then each to his own desire.''

"You don't appear to be very upset by anything today," Masuto said quite deliberately.

"Upset? You mean by Al's death?"

"And Tulley's murder."

"My goodness, Inspector, when you're a Mike Tulley you have to expect it, don't you? I mean, we used to watch the Perry Mason program on TV every now and then, and you always know who is going to get it, because it's the kind of person you feel so nasty about you could kill him yourself, and once I said to Murph that if we were running one of those programs in our own set, why it would be Mike Tulley, naturally.''

"Then you have no sympathy for Mike Tulley?"

"Goodness, I adored Mike. What has that got to do with him being a louse? If I had to eliminate every man who's a louse, I'd become a Vestal Virgin or something. Is that right? Vestal Virgin? You know, I dated Mike. When we were kid actors. Did you know that I was an actress, Inspector?"

It was thick, turgid. He was in a dream. She was playing with him or she was an idiot—or he was an idiot. The smile was fixed on her face, and her sharp, tiny white teeth reminded him of a cat's fangs. Every so often, she would touch her lips with the point of her tongue and leave them red and glistening—and then she would pass the back of a thumbnail across the velvet that covered her breasts.

"Oh, a very good actress indeed. Not that I ever really got a chance—don't you think I am a good actress, Inspector?" she asked archly.

"And weren't you moved by Mr. Greenberg's death?"

"Al was a sweetheart, but he was so sick, Inspector—so sick. You have no idea. Murph used to tell me that Al would sometimes stay up all night, he was so afraid of dying in his sleep. Well, that's one of the risks you take when you marry a popsie. Not that I haven't dated popsies, and there was one from Houston, Texas, who was worth a hundred million if he was worth a dime, but he could barely walk, and his doctor said he might live another ten years. Well, that's a long stretch for a girl to wait, Inspector. I know what you're thinking. You're thinking that Murph's a popsie, but that white hair of his puts you on. Murph was fifty last week, and I don't call that a popsie, not by a long shot. So Phoebe knew exactly what she was getting into, and who can cry over five million dollars—or whatever Al leaves Phoebe?"

At that moment, Masuto heard cars stopping outside, and Stacy rose and said wistfully, "Oh, there they are. And we were having such a wonderful chat, weren't we, Inspector?"

But in the first group were only Arlene Cotter and Trude Burke. The men had gone on to the other chapel where Mike Tulley's body lay, and when they returned with Lenore Tulley, it was almost ten o'clock. Then they waited for Phoebe Greenberg, who arrived a few minutes later.

But in the waiting time, Arlene Cotter and Trude Burke managed three drinks each. Arlene drank straight gin on the rocks, and Trude mixed brandy, sherry and ice. They sat in the enormous living room and grinned maliciously at Masuto. They begged him to take a drink.

"One little sip, Sarge," Arlene Cotter urged him. "I have never seen a Nipponese drunk."

"That's a real nasty thing to say," Stacy observed. As hostess, she forbore to actually drink, but instead nipped dainty sips from the sherry bottle. "You ought to apologize."

"Come to think of it," Trude observed, "you take a lot of garbage, don't you, Sarge?"

"All in a day's work," Masuto shrugged.

"What does it take to burn you?"

"I don't burn."

"Come on, Mr. Chan," Arlene said nastily, "everybody burns. It's not a question of susceptibility but a degree. Even our dark, comfortable little hostess here burns—right through the pretty pool of sherry that keeps her lit all day."

"How can you!" Stacy exclaimed dramatically.

"Because she's a bitch," Trude said. "It's easy enough, Stacy, if you only got a talent for it. Why be a louse, when with a little thought and effort you can be a thoroughgoing bitch like dear Arlene?"

"That's a lovely speech," Arlene replied, going to the bar and refurbishing her drink. "I've often wondered why Sidney never put you into the office, but I suppose your talents for public relations lie in other directions."

"Touché!" Trude grinned. "Did you hear it on TV or read it in a book?"

"Will you stop!" Stacy cried. "How do you think the Inspector feels? He's a guest in my house."

"Oh, climb down, Stacy," Arlene said. "You know, you give me a pain in the ass. That's crude—"

"Say that again," Trude agreed.

"—but there are times when crudity is obligatory," she went on, paying no attention to Trude. "In the first place, Mr. Chan is a sergeant, not an inspector. In the second place, he is not one bit bothered by anything we say here. He welcomes it, and he consideres himself very clever to be sitting there and waiting for the proper moment to pounce on some stupid remark we make."

"Then why don't you shut up," Trude said.

"Because I got nothing to hide from him, but with you the case is a horse of another color," Arlene said.

"My dear lady," Trude said, patting the pink curls that covered her head, "you don't even talk coherently, and before I'd crawl out on any limb and cut it off behind me, I'd think twice. Maybe three times. Because little old darling Arlene from New Orleans is maybe a little old sitting duck to Trude here."

"Stop it!" Stacy said again. Masuto felt that she was trying to weep with vexation and was equally frustrated by the fact that the tears would not come.

"Now she's insinuating that I don't come from New Orleans," Arlene said to Masuto, a trace of a Southern accent suddenly appearing in her voice. "But if I were married to Sidney Burke, I would stop insinuating. Because wherever I come from, doll, my husband doesn't practice a little pimping on the side."

"Balls," Trude said.

"What did you say?"

"You heard me, lovey. Because if there is any kind of pimping ever invented, dreamed of, or even speculated upon, Jack Cotter has had his finger in it. Sidney Burke may be a crumb, but at least he weighs in at one fifty and not at a ninth of a ton like that ex-Lothario butterball of yours."

"That's a beauty," Arlene said grandly. "I won't argue it—not for a moment. The truth is that Jack weighs two thirty, and most of it is hard bone and muscle and he could still break Sidney in two."

Stacy began to giggle. She stood in front of the bar, holding a tiny shot glass half full of sherry in her hand and giggling uncontrollably.

"What's gotten into you?" Arlene demanded.

"Oh, the two of you—you're just like two little girls in finishing school. And then they began boasting about how strong their daddies are—"

"What!" Arlene exclaimed.

"Finishing school!" Trude shouted.

"God save us!" Arlene cried.

"Say that again, lovey."

"Tell us more about finishing school."

"And your daddy, honeybunch."

"All the daddies that you used to boast about."

Masuto was watching them, but particularly watching Stacy. Her giggles stopped. She flung the shot glass at Arlene, missing her by a hair's breadth. Her body tensed. The softness left it. And under the black velvet dress, her body seemed to have the flowing strength of a giant cat, and her pale eyes flashed. Stacy thrust out one hand toward the two women, and spoke coldly and menacingly. "That's enough. I've had a bellyful of you two bitches! Now just shut up or I'll break your necks—both of you! And don't think I can't do it!"

Even Masuto recoiled from the supressed hate and violence of Stacy Anderson. Arlene Cotter and Trude Burke simply sat in their chairs and said nothing and stared at the rug.

And then the men arrived with Lenore Tulley, and shortly after that, Phoebe Greenberg arrived.

There was a corner arrangement in the living room of two big Lawson couches—both in red leather and brass studs—and four facing armchairs. Lenore Tulley and Phoebe Greenberg sat on one couch, and facing them, Sidney Burke, Arlene Cotter and Trude Burke. Sidney sat in the middle. Murphy Anderson had an armchair, and his wife, Stacy, hovered between the guests and the bar. Masuto was in another armchair and Cotter, self-appointed to begin the meeting, had wrapped himself over a cockfight chair and rocked gently as he faced the others. He was a big man, and while he ran to fat, Masuto agreed with Arlene that he could handle himself. He had that look about him. Masuto recalled him now in the old Westerns he had played, and thinking of those films, Masuto realized with a curious sense of hopelessness and resignation that like the others, he was a particular product of this thing called The United States, shaped by Westerns and other mythology; a strange, strange product of his time, a slant-eyed, dark-skinned, Zen-Buddhist–California-Yankee—a condition that made him shiver a bit. Still he responded to Cotter with some tinge of that ancient hero worship. Cotter was consciously playing a role now. The great Tudor room was the set, and as players, the circle of people he faced were both dramatic and interesting. Masuto had no doubt but that he had rehearsed an opening statement over and over; when he spoke, he said the line well.

"One of us," he told them, flatly and without emotion, "is a murderer."

There was an explosion of silence, a reaction Masuto understood very well indeed. Not one of the women said a word. Sidney Burke smiled self-consciously. Murphy Anderson shook his head slightly.

The silence stretched. It reached its breaking point. And Jack Cotter savored his moment. Then Stacy Anderson said crisply, "Jack, don't be an ass. These people are my friends. They are not murderers."

And Masuto asked himself, What will I tell my wife tomorrow then—that there are two women here I admire enormously? Of course he realized that he often chose strange people to admire. A man of prudence depended upon his own understanding more than upon his wife's.

"One of us is a murderer," Cotter repeated. "What's the use of horsing around? When I said that poor Al was murdered, the doctors pooh-poohed the whole thing. Well, I say, let's face it. You knew damn well, when Murph asked us here, just what we had in mind."

"Did I know it too, Jack?" Phoebe inquired.

"Let's stop beating around the bush. In one way or another, we all knew it. Aside from Sergeant Masuto, there are eight of us here, and one of the eight is a killer. Seven came because they had a genuine desire to see the killer exposed. The killer came because if she didn't come, she would give herself away."

"She?" Stacy Anderson raised a brow.

"Come on, Stacy—enough."

"And what does that mean?"

"It means that you know as well as I do that we're dealing with a woman," Jack Cotter said. "Mr. Masuto will bear witness to that." He turned to Masuto and demanded, "Am I right, Sergeant?"

"That I will bear witness to your statement?"

"Exactly."

"But how can I, Mr. Cotter? Do you think I know who the killer is?" The others were watching him intently now, and Masuto allowed his narrowed eyes to scan their faces.

"I think you have a damn good notion who the killer is."

"Suppose we were to grant that," Masuto said. "Suppose we were to grant that, simply for the sake of argument—and understand that I will accept your contention on no other basis. Suppose we say that I have a damn good notion of who the murder is? What could I do with a damn good notion, as you put it? It's not proof. It will not stand up in any court of law. And if I had any real proof, do you imagine that I would have come to a charade like this? I think that you and Mr. Anderson have read too many murder mysteries, sir."

"That's a hell of a note!" Cotter snapped. "I think you got one hell of a goddamn nerve, mister—"

"Oh, hold on, hold on, Jack," Murphy Anderson said. "Just take it easy. I was dubious about this idea in the first place, and I agreed to go along and give it a try because you were so certain that it would bring some results. But the fact of the matter is that Detective Masuto is right. We have no proof, and we have no right to keep anyone here who desires to leave. All we have is about seven yards of insinuations.''

"Is that so," said Sidney Burke, rising abruptly. "Well, as far as I am concerned, some of these suspicions and insinuations got to be busted wide up."

"Oh, Sidney, sit down and don't be such a cockamamie schmuck," Trude said.

"Like hell I will. I am going to say my piece."

"Well, there it is," Trude sighed, spreading her arms. "He is going to say his piece."

"And to you too," he snapped, turning on Trude.

"I'm all ears."

"God damn it, Sidney," Anderson said, "whatever you got to say—say it and let's not have a family squabble."

"Oh, Murph doll, you are dreaming if you think we won't have family squabbles tonight," Arlene said. "By the dozen—believe me."

"You weary me so, why don't you shut up!" Trude said.

"All right—all of you!" Cotter ordered. "Now say your piece, Sidney."

"OK. I don't have to go into the Samantha thing again. You know about that bitch. Now I am going to be sincere— fully sincere, and let the pieces fall where they may. I was driving on Mulholland today, and I passed Trude in her MG going in the other direction. I went on and came on the accident. You all know about the accident by now. A onetime stripper named Peggy Groton went over the shoulder and was killed. The Sarge was there. He's on this case, but he was there in LA—and I say the two cases connect. You don't have to be no genius for that. I spoke to you and Murph about it before," he said to Cotter, "and you agreed with me. The two cases got to connect."

"Not necessarily," Masuto said.

"Then what in hell were you doing up there on Mulholland Drive in Los Angeles?"

"I have friends in the LA Police Department," Masuto told them. "Pete Bones is the name of one of them. I had business with him. I found him up there at the accident."

"Well, what about that, Sidney?" Anderson asked seriously.

"What about it? Does it account for the fact that I passed Trude driving away from the scene of the accident?"

Now Trude was on her feet. "Do you know what that crumby little bastard is trying to do?" she cried. "I'll tell you what he's trying to do! He's trying to set me up for the gas chamber! He's trying to finger me as Samantha! Does that make a record or does it not? My own husband fingering me for murder!"

"Take it easy," Anderson said. "No one is fingering you for any murder."

"Murph, for Christ's sake, open your eyes and stop being a calm, objective lawyer!" his wife shouted. "It's bad enough to have to live in the same town as Sidney Burke. Now I got him under my own roof talking like the little pisspot he is!"

"Oh, that's fine language!" Anderson exclaimed. "That's real fine language."

"The hell with my language," Stacy shouted. "Next thing, he'll open a cathouse in the maid's room."

"Sure, you're a dame!" Sidney yelled back at her. "Go ahead. Call me anything you like. I'm gentleman enough not to bat you one."

"Shut up—all of you!" Cotter roared. "You're all behaving like a bunch of delinquent kids. Now just shut up for one lousy cotton-picking moment!"

A sort of silence prevailed. Sidney took a turn away from the couch and stopped to lean against the bar. Trude sank back into the couch. Phoebe watched Masuto, who sat back in his chair, breathing softly and evenly, his face blank, composed, receptive. Murphy took out a handkerchief and wiped his face, and Stacy walked to the bar and poured herself a shot glass half full of sherry. She ignored Sidney, and Masuto considered it as fine a job of ignoring as he had ever seen. His respect for Stacy Anderson rose another notch, and he considered how it would be to spend an evening with her. Just an evening, he assured himself.

"Anyone want a drink?" she asked.

"Give me a sherry and dry vermouth on the rocks," Lenore said. "It's intermission. Do you know they sell liquor in the New York theatres now—between the acts?"

"Just like London," Arlene Cotter said.

"Then you've been to London, darling," Lenore said. "What a well-travelled, cultured little dear you are!"

"Enough of that," Cotter told her. "Let's cut out this backbiting and get to the center of things." He addressed himself to Trude. "Where were you today between twelve noon and twelve-thirty?"

Trude laughed. "You are a lulu, Jack. The ever-living end, aren't you?"

"I am going to repeat that question," Cotter said. "Where were you today between twelve and twelve-thirty?"

"Drop dead, lover boy."

"You refuse to answer?"

"Are you nuts?" Trude demanded. "I don't have to answer your stupid questions. Where do you come off putting your nose into my business? You want this Samantha of yours—go find her. But I don't have to answer any of your stupid questions." She turned to Masuto. "Do I?"

"Not if you don't want to," Masuto said.

"Well, then, you ask her the question," Cotter told Masuto.

"She doesn't have to answer me either."

"What? You mean you can ask her questions, and she can tell you to go run around the block?"

"Exactly."

Cotter turned to Anderson. "Murph—is that so?"

"That's so. I don't know what the hell you expect to accomplish here tonight, Jack."

"You poor jerks really think I am Samantha?" Trude said.

"They think we're all Samantha," Stacy said.

"Stacy!" Anderson protested.

"It's true, isn't it?"

"I've had enough of this," Arlene Cotter said. "I am going home before I start thinking about this crew we married and throw up."

"Stick around, lovey," Trude said. "If you walk out, they'll pin it on you."

"What I can't understand," Jack Cotter said to Masuto, "is why, now that we're all here together, you don't start asking questions and rooting out the truth."

"Because there's no truth in that."

"Don't tell me that!"

"Mr. Cotter," Masuto said softly, "suppose I began to ask questions, as you suggest. No one has to answer."

"Then when they don't answer, you got guilt."

"Is she guilty then?" the detective asked, pointing to Trude. "Because if she is, then our search is over."

"I didn't say she was guilty."

"Don't even infer it," Trude said, smiling pleasantly. "Because, Jackie dear, we are not inside some silly novel but here in this room and surrounded with witnesses. That jackass, my husband, over there by the bar, has already practically called me a murderer. But he is my husband, and so long as he pulls down better than six figures a year, he remains my husband. But you, Jackie, you ain't my husband, and just make one lousy crack about me and I will sue you for defamation of character so hard you'll be knocking at the gates of the actors' old age home. I'll sue you for every nickle you got, so don't go pushing the Sarge to ask me questions."

"Can she do that?" Cotter demanded of Anderson.

"I'm afraid so."

"I never called you a murderer. That's for the record. I want everyone here a witness to that fact. I never called you a murderer."

"Just what did you think you would accomplish with all this?" Stacy asked him.

"You know what I think," Sidney Burke said suddenly. "I think the company should hire the best private eyes here on the coast. We get as many privates as we need, and we blow this thing wide open. That's my sincere position."

"I don't believe it," Stacy said with disgust.

"Sidney is Sidney," Phoebe said tiredly, speaking for the first time. "He's been around for fifteen years, and suddenly, big deal, you discover that he's a louse. How about you and Murph?" she asked Cotter. "Aren't you lice? Aren't you the worst pair of lice that ever drove a pair of convertible Cadillacs in Beverly Hills? And you, Stacy—dear old Stacy."

"I'm willing to forget what you just said," Anderson told her. "You've had too much stress."

"I think we have all had too much stress," Stacy Anderson agreed. "We have all talked too much and said too much—which perhaps was exactly what our dear Mr. Masuto wanted."

"Not at all," Masuto said.

"Then why have you come?"

"I was asked to come."

"And only that? And that's why you've been sitting there all evening like a superior cat waiting to select the proper mouse to eat?"

"That's a very poetic image, Mrs. Anderson, but I am not a psychological detective. I am only a policeman in plainclothes."

"Then just what do you propose?" Cotter demanded. "That Murph and Sidney and I just sit on our hands and patiently allow ourselves to be murdered?"

"What, only the three of you? Why not the women?" Masuto asked.

"And you're not putting us on?" Sidney complained. "Oh, no—no, you're not putting us on, not one bit. Three men in this outfit are scragged, and you ask why the men."

"How about Peggy Groton?" Masuto said.

"Who's Peggy Groton?"

"The dead are quickly forgotten, aren't they?"

"She's the dame on Mulholland Drive," Cotter said.

"Anyway," Anderson said, "it seems that we three men are the most likely sitting ducks. Don't you agree with that, Mr. Masuto?"

"Possibly."

"Look," Anderson continued, "I have been thinking about this all evening, and I see no reason why Jack's statement should be taken at face value."

"What statement?" Cotter demanded.

"That the murderer is here in this room. How do we know that this Samantha is here? She might have never come near any of us. She might be a maid in someone's home. She might be a typist or secretary at the office. She might work on the set. The point I am making is that she might be anywhere."

"Haven't you worked over that Samantha business sufficiently?" Phoebe Greenberg said.

Stacy Anderson then turned to Masuto and said, "My dear policeman, since you refuse to question us, may I question you?"

"By all means." Masuto smiled.

"Where is this Samantha that these three dirty old men can't unhook from?"

"I have no idea."

"Does she exist?"

"I don't know."

"Oh, you are a great crystal ball. Is the murderer in this room? Jack says yes, Murph says no. Well?"

"Yes."

"What do you mean, yes? You're breaking your track record."

"You asked me whether the murderer is in this room. I said yes. The murderer is in this room."

"Then why don't you arrest him?"

The whole place tightened now. Masuto could hear their breathing, the difference in quality, the softness of some, the rasping quality of others. Sidney and Arlene lit cigarettes. The thin threads of smoke curled among the group.

"It is very interesting," Masuto observed, "that when a man speaks of the killer he designates him as a woman, and when a woman speaks of the murderer, she designates him as a man. There would be a neutral designation in a society as complex as ours—wouldn't you say? Some criminologists hold that murder never occurs without the presence of homosexuality—"

"Who the hell needs philosophy?" Cotter snapped.

"I don't like this talk about faggots," Sidney said. "To me, a man is what he is. That's all. That's my sincere feeling. A man is what he is. That's the way you judge him."

"You were asked a question, Sergeant Masuto," Murphy Anderson said. "You said you knew who the murderer is. Then you were asked why you don't arrest the murderer."

"No. Not at all," said Masuto. "I was not asked whether I knew who the murderer is. I was asked whether the murderer is in this room. I answered in the affirmative."

"Then I am asking you. Who is the murderer?"

Masuto waited for a long moment before he replied. No one moved. Each and every one of them there in that room was completely self-conscious about not moving.

"There are two reasons why I don't answer that," Masuto said. "First, I am not certain, not totally certain. Three men and a woman have been murdered. The murderer has been a fool, but a lucky fool. But this is a monstrous crime, and there must be certainty before I make the accusation. Second, I must have proof. An arrest is meaningless without proof.''

"And until you get this proof?'' Cotter demanded. "Do we just wait and die?''

They were all beginning to relax—as if the accusation of any one of them there and then would have been more than they could take.

"No. I think the case is breaking.''

"Just what do you mean by that?'' Anderson asked.

"There was a witness to one of the murders,'' Masuto said. He had been holding it all evening and waiting to drop it. He dropped it now. He dropped it almost casually and watched them.

Nothing. They tightened as a group, and they watched him.

"Which murder?'' Cotter asked finally.

"Fred Saxton—your production manager who was killed by a counterweight seven weeks ago. That would appear to be a nearly perfect murder, but like every nearly perfect act it faces too many imponderables. One of them was this woman.''

"What woman?'' Trude asked softly.

"Just an actress, a character actress, age fifty-one, not too much work, only now and then. She lives. She has a husband. She minds her own business.''

"Who is she?'' Stacy asked sharply.

"How does she come into this?'' Anderson wanted to know.

"She was a witness, Mr. Anderson,'' Masuto said. "The day Fred Saxton was killed, she wandered over to Stage 6. No reason for it. There is never any reason for the imponderables. She had been standing by for hours waiting for her take, and she was bored. So she poked into Stage 6 out of idle curiosity, and she saw someone with a hand on the rope release. Then the counterweight fell and Saxton was dead. In the excitement that followed, she slipped away. But as the day wore on she became aware of all the details involved, and being a reasonably intelligent woman, she put two and two together and came up with murder. But being a timid woman, she did what a great many people would do. She decided to keep her mouth shut and not get involved."

"And when did she change her mind?" Phoebe asked coldly, staring at Masuto. Their eyes met.

"Today, of course," Masuto replied.

"Why?"

"Because she heard about Mike Tulley's murder, and she put two and two and two together, and she called the Los Angeles police. They put a call out for me and we talked. They agreed to let me do it my way, because the Beverly Hills need took preference."

"And what is your way?" Anderson asked.

"Very simple, very direct. She's working out at World Wide tomorrow—you do have a permanent lease on Stage 6?" he asked Anderson.

"Not permanent, but we have it for another ten days. There's nothing shooting there now. We wound up our work there after Freddie's death. We made an arrangement with Grapheonics to keep their tour costumes there."

"What is Grapheonics?" Masuto asked.

"They're an animated cartoon outfit. 'Captain Devildom,' 'Space Ace Ambrose,' 'Major Meridean,' 'Tentacle Horror,' 'Captain Sharkman'—they have a slew of things that the kids eat up. Four to five on prime kiddie time. They've been so successful that World Wide asked them to become a part of the tour."

"The tour?"

"The 'studio tour.' They have those motor buses, you know, little open things, and they take tourists all over the sets and sound stages and the back lot. It's been enormously successful—so much so that they incorporated into the tour the characters from Grapheonics—in costume, of course. World Wide likes it and Grapheonics likes it, and we allow Grapheonics to keep their costumes on Stage 6—in the wardrobe there. It's convenient for them. Just a gesture on our part."

"That won't interfere with my plan," Masuto said. "I would like all of us to get together tomorrow on Stage 6 at about ten minutes to eleven in the morning. Then I'll bring her to Stage 6, and she'll pick out the murderer."

"Just like that," Anderson said coldly.

"It's very simple. Yes. Just like that."

"And your murderer will come there like a lamb to the slaughter?"

"What alternative does the murderer have, Mr. Anderson?"

"I don't buy it!" Sidney Burke declared shrilly. "I don't buy it. It's a lousy, stupid scheme and I don't want any part of it. I have tried to be sincere through this whole crumby business, but now I've had a bellyful!"

"Sidney," Trude said sweetly.

"Now you listen to me—" he began.

"Oh, no—no, you cockamamie idiot, you listen to me. A moment ago, you were calling me a murderer. But let's lay it on the line. You're too stupid to be Samantha, even if you had enought guts to be a woman, which you haven't. So no one here is going to think you are the killer. We both go to World Wide tomorrow, and we wind this business up. Once and for all, because I don't intend to live with it another day."

"I second that," Jack Cotter said. "The Sergeant makes sense. Do you agree?" he asked his wife.

Arlene shrugged. "I'm just along for the ride."

"Al's funeral is tomorrow," Anderson reminded them. "I don't see how Phoebe is going to get there."

"Can't we leave Phoebe out of this?" Stacy asked. "I just can't cast her as some bloody, maniacal killer."

"Then suppose you leave me out, cookie," Lenore said. "My alibi is as good as hers." She looked around from face to face. "And just in case you forget, I have my own dead to bury."

"Darling," said Arlene, "that line goes so much better in the original with Bogart than second hand with you."

"Go to hell!"

Phoebe looked at Masuto, who nodded just the slightest bit, and then Phoebe said, "I'll come. The funeral's in the afternoon, and if poor Al won't rest easier, at least I'll shed a few tears less for knowing who did it and why."

"Sidney?" Murphy asked.

"All right. I'm in the middle of this. I'm trying to be sincere—so I'm the number one louse. I'll be there."

"I'll be with him," Trude said.

"If I'm not dead," Sidney said. "I got to live through the night. Remember that."

"My heart bleeds for you."

"I just bet."

"All right, Sergeant," Anderson said, running his fingers nervously through his thick white hair. "We're agreed, we'll be there, and God help all of us."

Masuto followed Phoebe home. The cop on duty outside of her house was alert, and before Masuto had taken three steps, there was a gun in his ribs, and a harsh voice inquired, "What's wrong with the path, buster?"

He had deliberately stepped over the low hedge by the driveway to move through the shrubs in front of the veranda. A moment later the cop recognized him and apologized, and Masuto said, "Never mind the apologies. You guard this place as if it were Fort Knox."

"I'll do that, Sarge."

Masuto rang the front doorbell, and Phoebe opened the door herself.

"Don't open doors!" he snapped. "You have servants."

"Don't order me around either, Mr. Masuto. I have had my fill of you. You're a liar."

"I am, you are—" He walked into the entranceway,

and she closed the door behind him. "We're all liars. I lie for my work. That's not a matter of morality."

"But it is morality to set me up like a sheep for slaughter. Or is that in the line of good police work."

He stared at her for a long moment, and then he shook his head. "Oh, no—Mrs. Greenberg. You misjudge me. I am a happily married man, but I have met a few women in my life who make me wonder whether being happily married is enough. You are one of them. You are a fine and beautiful woman—"

She burst out laughing. "Dear man," she said.

"Did I say something stupid."

She began to cry now. He gave her his handkerchief. "It's clean," he said. "I haven't used it today. But what have I done to make you cry?"

She shook her head.

"I am not risking your life," he said definitely. "There will be studio policemen there, both armed—two good men that we can count on. Nothing will happen to you."

"I don't care."

"But you must care."

"There's really not one damned thing left to care about."

"There's the world to live in," he said. "To live in it and taste it and feel it—open your eyes to it."

"Don't preach to me."

He shook his head. She seemed to sway, and then he took her in his arms. Afterwards, he wondered whether the act was of specific volition or not. He only held her against him, tightly, for one long moment. He didn't kiss her, and when a moment later he loosed his arms and she stepped back away from him, he felt a sense of awful loss. He had not kissed her. The embrace was not an embrace. A wind of foolish memory blew away what had never been, and he stood there feeling bereft and stupid.

She handed him his handkerchief. It had lipstick on it. He knew he would throw it away. He had no desire to try to explain to his wife why it had lipstick on it.

"I am sorry, Mrs. Greenberg," he said.

"Would you try to call me Phoebe, just once. Or don't you like the name?"

"It's a beautiful name."

"Then please call me Phoebe."

"Very well. I am sorry, Phoebe."

"For what?"

"For embracing you."

"Would you just tell me why you should be sorry because you embraced me?"

"There are three reasons, Phoebe. One, I am a cop. Two, I am a Nisei. Three, I am married. Perhaps a fourth reason more important than any—that you are Al Greenberg's widow."

"Oh, don't be such a precious damned fool! I loved my husband. I think I would have died for him, if need be—but not as a husband, and he never expected me to love him as a husband. But that's beside the point. You didn't even make a pass at me. You don't want to, and I don't want you to, and I do wish that you would stop acting like something out of a Japanese print. You're a man—a strong man who is reasonably decent and who turns up on the one day of my life when I need a man desperately. If things were different—"

"But they are not different," Masuto said.

"No, they are not different, are they? What is your first name?"

"Masao."

"Very well. Then from here on until the end of this, you call me Phoebe and I will call you Masao. Is that agreed? Openly. Right?"

"I will call you Phoebe, and you will call me Masao."

"As good friends should."

"As good friends should," he repeated.

Then he left. On his way home, he threw away the handkerchief, just as he had known that he would.

CHAPTER EIGHT

Gertrude Bestner

When Masuto entered his home in Culver City, his wife was waiting, her face drawn. She was an anxious mother. The house and her family were her world and all the world that she wanted, and she stubbornly refused to be Americanized. There were times when Masuto took great pleasure in this, and usually her anxieties were flattering to his own strength. But he had his own anxieties now, and he listened with some irritation to her story of Michael, the eight-year-old son, and his sore throat. Apparently, the sore throat was worse.

"Did you go to the doctor?" he asked.

She looked at him reproachfully. They had one car and she did not drive. She was always promising to learn to drive.

"Then why didn't you call the doctor to come here?"

"That's ten dollars, Masao. If I call the doctor every time a kid has a sore throat, we'll soon be penniless."

"We are penniless, the way you watch every dollar!"

"Masao!"

She always knew when something happened inside of him. It was not the things that occurred outside of him that worried her, but the strange responses that sometimes overtook him. That was the way it was tonight. In bed she left a space between their bodies, and when he whispered to her, she pretended that she was asleep.

Sleep came hard to him. He would doze off and come awake again. He dreamed of being lost in strange places—jungles and cities and boundless plains—but in each and every place there was Beverly Hills. Yet finally, he fell fully asleep and slept until the alarm awakened him at seven in the morning.

This morning, he was more than solicitous of his wife, Kati. He went out of his way to help her with the smallest child and then he made the seven wonderful faces for Michael, who would spend the day in bed. He was almost ready to leave when the telephone rang. Kati answered it. Masuto was outside the kitchen door when she called him, "It's Pete Bones."

He came back and picked up the phone and said, "Masao, Pete. I'm on my way out."

"Well, just hold still for a moment. We got a make on Gertrude Bestner."

"Who?"

"Oh, no—no, I don't believe it. You only give us the life and death howl, and research works fifteen hours straight, and now you ask me, who is Gertrude Bestner."

"Wait—you mean Samantha Adams, nee Gertrude Bestner?"

"Exactly."

"You mean you've found her?"

"In a manner of speaking," Bones said. "All that's mortal. She's buried in the County Pauper's Reserve."

"Dead."

"Very dead, Masao."

"You know—funny thing, but I felt it. The poor kid was a loser."

"Maybe."

"When did she die?" Masuto asked.

"Nineteen fifty-six, age nineteen, pneumonia, Mt. Sinai Hospital, emergency case; picked her up in the street where she had fainted; malnutrition, semistarvation, pulmonary—she died seven hours after admission to the hospital. Her death certificate was signed by the ward resident, name of Harry Levine. Practices medicine in Brentwood. I have name, address and telephone. Do you want it?''

''No,'' said Masuto.

''Funny thing, Masao, when she was admitted she gave them the name of Samantha Adams—the way these kids cling to the dream that it's theirs to make big, real big. It wasn't until she died that they got her real name from the ID in her purse.''

''Where did she come from?''

''Chicago—but no connection, no family, no nearest of kin, nothing. A kid dies and it's like she's never been. Jesus, there are times when you could take this job and shove it right up your ever-loving.''

''It's not the job, it's just the way things are,'' Masuto said.

''I suppose so. Look, we got her effects from the morgue file. Not much. A purse, a few incidentals—you know what a kid keeps with her—and a little leather-bound day book with a few phone numbers and some diary entries.''

''Have you checked the phone numbers?''

''Aside from agencies and the unions and that kind of thing, they're all discontinued. She's got the number of Sidney Burke's PR outfit, but I guess you expected that.''

''I expected it,'' Masuto said. ''Did you read everything?''

''Well, it wasn't no *War and Peace*. Sure, I read it all.''

''Anything?''

''Well, it depends on what you want. I got it here in front of me. On December 25th, 1955, she wrote, 'This is Xmas. It's a lousy Xmas. That's all I can say. It's a lousy, lousy Xmas. I had no date on Xmas Eve, and I walked around and I walked up the Strip and I almost began to cry for feeling sorry for myself. Then I walked over to Fairfax and I bought a fruit cake for thirty-five cents. That left me with eighteen cents, but I had to have something even for a lousy Xmas like this. So I went home and stuffed myself with the fruit cake. It wasn't much good. It wasn't anything like the fruit cakes Mrs. Walensky used to make in Chi. They were great fruit cakes. God, I wish I was a kid again. I don't. It was lousy to be a kid. But God, I wish I was a kid again. Today, I'm sitting here in my room waiting for Santa Claus. This is Samantha, Santa Claus. Wishing you a lousy merry Xmas—' ''

"That's enough," said Masuto.

"There's more. A million laughs."

"Go to hell."

"That's a fine way to thank a buddy. Do you know what I told the boss—I told him to bill Beverly Hills for the time spent. You can afford it. You can afford to pave your streets with two-bit pieces."

"I'll tell them that at City Hall."

"Do you want to look at this stuff?"

"No."

"At least be grateful."

"Thanks," said Masuto. He replaced the telephone and then stood there staring at it.

"Masao," his wife said.

Not moving, he stared at the telephone. Perhaps not hearing, because she asked him again, "Masao, please, what happened? Did something terrible happen?"

"Yes."

"What?"

"A girl died. A little girl died."

"How awful! Is it someone close to you? Who is it?"

"I don't know her. I never saw her."

"I don't understand."

"She died ten years ago, and they buried her in a pauper's grave. Her name was Samantha. That was her stage name. Her real name was Gertrude Bestner, and in the whole world today, maybe only Pete Bones and I speak that name aloud."

"Samantha. Pete Bones. What strange names the Anglos use!"

"Anglos?"

"You don't like the word?"

"I don't know. It's just a word. We're not Mexicans."

"Is it a word only for the Mexicans? What do we call them?"

"People. Just people. That's enough."

"You're in a strange mood," she said. "This case has changed you. When will it be over?"

"Today, I think."

"Oh, God—Masao—"

"I will be in no danger," he said impatiently. "Nothing will happen to me. We will have a good dinner tonight, and I will tell you all about it."

"And it will be over?"

"All over and done with. I promise you that, and then I can go back to being a Beverly Hills policeman."

"And tomorrow is your day off," she said with delight. "We can have a picnic."

"If Michael is well enough."

"And where will we go, Masao?"

"To San Fernando, I think, to Soko's place. He promised that he would have the Sashu Roses from Japan. They are new, quite small, almost a mustard color, and they have a very good strong smell. I am tired of these new beautiful tea roses that have no scent. We will eat in his garden, and then I will bring home the rose bushes and plant them."

"Good. Good."

He kissed her and went out to the car. The windshield was blurred with the wet morning mist, and upon it, in big block letters, he traced out SAMANTHA. Then he wiped it away with the palm of his hand, and then got in the car and drove off.

CHAPTER NINE

Frank Jefferson

In the mood that gripped him this morning, Masuto was unable to face the freeway with its maniacal roar of seventy-mile-an-hour traffic, and he decided to take a few minutes longer on his journey to the Valley and World Wide Studios by going through Beverly Drive to Coldwater Canyon. He was glad that he did. This was one of those utterly improbable Los Angeles mornings when there is neither smog nor fog and the air is as sharp and as clean as crystal. When he passed over the rise of Coldwater, the Valley lay etched below him, so clean and clear that he imagined he could see San Fernando in the distance.

Almost, the Valley reminded him of the way it had been when he was just a kid, with its acres of orange grove and mango grove and avocado and pecan, its woods and stately avenues of eucalyptus and little brooks and Mexican and Japanese farmers, its tiny towns, its fiestas and roadside picnic places. Scattered around the Valley were relatives and friends. Masuto's father then had an old, old Model A Ford, and when it was loaded with venerable family and grinning children, it was always a great adventure to see whether it could puff and grind its way over wonderful Coldwater Canyon Road.

All that gone—and overnight. The proliferating hundred-thousand-dollar houses had turned Coldwater into a sort of street, and every inch of the Valley below was subdivided and covered with frantically built wooden houses. The orchards were gone and the ranches were gone. Thirty thousand dollars an acre was a price no farmer could resist, and most of the year its green wetness lay under a cover of yellow, noxious smog.

He pushed all this away from him, telling himself that he was only a cop and that too much halfbaked philosophy was notoriously bad for policemen. And then, when he reached Ventura Boulevard, he deliberately went on to the freeway and raced over the last few miles to World Wide Studios at seventy miles an hour, as any proper Southern Californian should.

It was not yet nine o'clock in the morning, but the vast sprawling studio was already awake and working: the stream of extras parking their cars in the great expanse of the employees' lot, the stars parking their Ferraris and Rollses and Thunderbirds in the few precious shaded spots; the little studio electrics shunting back and forth; the grips and carpenters and electricians walking from their cars to the stages where they would work this morning; the executives, the producers and directors, halting in little groups of emphatic importance; the office workers pouring into the cafeteria for the cup of coffee they missed at home; the writers dragging their feet, bowed in the inevitable gloom of their profession; the cowboys and badmen and Civil War soldiers and gowned and beribboned ladies giving that final and delightful sense of color to the gigantic dream-factory—all of it a never-ending wonder to Masuto.

He always watched and reacted; it was always new and exciting. He waved to the guards at the gate as he drove in, and he preempted one of the spaces marked off for security and then he walked over to the security cottage, where Frank Jefferson presided. Frank Jefferson was a grizzled man in his middle sixties, a onetime cop, onetime head of one of the largest private detective agencies on the West Coast, and now, at a better salary than he had ever earned, in charge of the private police force of forty uniformed and un-uniformed men who guarded World Wide Studios.

He sat back in his swivel chair now, his feet—in the low, embossed cowboy boots he affected—up on his desk, and regarded Masuto with interest and respect.

"Masao," he said, "you are not the model of a public servant. You got a mind in that noodle of yours. Come out here and I'll start you at twelve thousand. A year from now you'll head up my plainclothes division at eighteen thousand. What do you say?"

Masuto smiled and shook his head.

"All right, the hell with it. No cop really has brains, or what for would he be a cop? What can I do for you?"

"Got fifteen minutes?"

"I got the whole morning if you need it." He opened his intercom and said to the girl outside, "Bubby, hold any calls, and if you do it real nice, I'll give you a brand new set of black lace panties I got in my drawer."

He grinned at Masuto. "Lousy sense of humor, huh? But I got a good reputation. I stopped patting behinds five years ago, so I can say anything I want to. I'm an eccentric—just like you, Masao. For half a century I been a coarse old bastard, but now I'm an eccentric. How about that?"

"It's an improvement."

"Ah! Like hell it is! It's a case of gonadal decay. Now what can I do for the police force of Beverly Hills?"

Masuto told him. He told him the entire story, and Jefferson listened with interest and approval.

"Pretty good," he said when Masuto had finished. "Pretty damn good."

"You agree with me?"

"Well! That's the question, isn't it? As a cop, Masao, I am inclined to agree. As a member of the jury, I don't convict on what you got. It's a series of indications but not evidence. The curse of a cop is no different from the curse of the world—subjectivity. Like you, I liked Al Greenberg.

He was direct, simple, and kind—and if that ain't unusual in this business, I don't know what is. It's too easy to get mad at the thought of some swine knocking him over that way. As for Mike Tulley—well, I'll tell you. With actors it's this way, you either like them or you don't. Same as with kids. You either like kids or you don't, and if you don't there's nothing a kid can do that's right. Myself, I like actors. I know what they are. They are vain, narcissistic, totally self-absorbed, selfish, self-pitying, self-indulgent, and maybe a few other things. They are also generous, outgoing, emotional and sometimes the best kind of people to have around. So maybe I'll cry a few tears over Mike Tulley—and you might too. So judgement is not to be trusted one hundred percent. I think you're right, but even if you are wrong, it's good odds that you'll smoke out the bastard responsible for all this. I don't like the thought of a murder at World Wide. I don't like the thought that a killer can operate in this studio with impunity. God knows, you got enough going in a studio to give any cop gray hair just in the ordinary run of things. I don't want any carte blanche for murder, and I like to keep my own house clean. Now what do you want from me?''

"Can you take a walk over to Stage 6?" Masuto asked.

"All right."

They walked across the studio grounds toward Stage 6. Jefferson wore a big, expensive, pearl-colored Stetson, a sport coat with gray checks, and he packed a forty-five caliber revolver in a shoulder holster. "Protective coloration," he had once told Masuto. "It makes me a part of the place." But he was consciously a character, a big man, well over six feet. He knew everyone and said hello to everyone.

"Always let them underestimate you, Masao," he said. "But you know that as well as I do."

Stage 6 was a large, cement-covered square block of a building. It completed a street of stages and processing houses, and then there was a big open space, bounded on

three sides with stages and storerooms, but open on the
fourth side to the thousand-acre stretch of sage and mesquite-
covered hills that made up the vast back lot of World Wide
Studios. Up in those hills was all that was necessary to the
operation of a modern, contained studio: ranches, block-
houses, frontier forts, Indian villages, lakes, rivers, falls,
sections of steamboats, an African village, a French town,
a medieval castle, a casbah, a New York street scene, a
London street scene, alpine peaks, cliffs—all of it linked
by a winding, improbable road which was the basis for the
studio tour.

"This square," said Jefferson, "is the first stop for the
tour. You know, star's dressing room, soundstage—they
go through Stage 11, over there. Then they snoop through
the carpentry shop and the plaster shop. Neither shop does
the real work anymore. We've moved the main effort over
to West Studio, but we still do enough here to give it a
feeling of validity. This tour gives me a headache, and I'll
have to put on six or seven extra men, but it is still the
most original piece of entertainment anyone has thought of
for a long time. Well, like I said, all the tour cars stop
here. There's the first one coming now."

He pointed down the studio street to where a gaily
painted bus of sorts had appeared. An open bus, its seats
stretched full across like the seats in a San Francisco
cable car, with front, back and sides, were open except for
a striped yellow and black awning. The awning was supported by six upright posts. The bus carried some twenty-
four people. There was no question but that they were
out-of-state sightseers. They wore sport shirts, carried
cameras, and ran strongly to old folks and children; and
they had the incredibly innocent, ready-to-believe look of
people transported to some place as unlikely as the moon.

"The bus is a six-cylinder GM special job, geared very
low," Jefferson said. "The best it can do is twenty miles
an hour, but on that one-lane road, that's more than enough.
There are hairpin turns up there on the mountain that you

wouldn't want to joyride over. Well, enough of that. You want to bring your kids out here for the tour, I'll get them passes."

"That's good of you," Masuto said.

"It is, bubby. Even the studio executives pay. Now let's get down to cases. Here's Stage 6. What do you want me to do?"

"You understand, Frank, that I can't map out all that's going to happen. Maybe nothing will happen. Maybe our killer knows it's a bluff."

"Maybe."

"But the odds are that I was believed, and if I was believed, the killer is as cool as ice and will plan to take out the witness. The killer is insane, and therefore the plan will be somewhat insane. Now we cannot anticipate the plan, but we can lay down certain rules for the game. Phoebe Greenberg will be outside. By the way—where will she make up?"

"They got their makeup department on Stage 9. They're shooting two pilots, one on Stage 9 and the other on Stage 10, but they coordinate the makeup and do it all on Stage 9. The makeup girl there is Jesse Klein, a real bubby. Why don't we walk over and talk to her?"

"Good enough." They started over to Stage 9. "She comes over from Stage 9 to Stage 6. By then, I'll have the whole lot of them, with the exception of Phoebe, in Stage 6."

"If they show."

"They'll show. You can be sure of that. Now here's what I mean when I say that I can lay down certain rules for the game. I tell them that they must stay on stage—that under no condition is anyone to leave the stage until I return. Then I go outside and meet Phoebe. Then, when I have left, one of them will find some way to evade the others and get out of the soundstage."

"Won't the others miss him right off?"

"No. The place is too big—and they're all mavericks.

They won't stay together no matter what I tell them. Leave it to our killer to work it out."

"This is a mighty iffy business, bubby," Jefferson said.

"Of course it is. But what other way can we play it? I must gamble that only one of them will come out—and that's our cookie. How many doors does the stage have?"

"The hangar doors are locked. On the side facing the street, there are two doors, one at each corner. Then there's the alley, with a third door. That's the side alley. Back alley has two fire exits from the flying bridges and outside fire escapes."

"Is there anything about this studio that you don't know?" Masuto asked.

"Very little, bubby—very little. If they pay me thirty-five thousand a year to walk around here in a cowboy hat, there's got to be a reason why."

"All right. I come out of that door—the one nearest us." They were at Stage 9 now, and Masuto pointed across the big square to Stage 6. "So that's covered. I want a man in the street to cover the other street door. I want a man in the alley, and I want a man behind the building to cover the fire exits. That's three men. Got them?"

"They're yours. When?"

"I want them behind the building at ten forty. On the nose. I'll meet them there."

"You got it. What else?"

"I want them armed."

"They're armed. But I don't want any shooting, Masao. They're good men and they know how to use their hands and they carry billies. I got a clean record on this lot. We never had shooting, not in the eighteen years I been here, and I don't want any now."

"The killer will be armed."

"Then if a gun is pulled, it's up to them to get the drop. Don't worry about that. When your killer shows, they will control the situation. I told you they're good men."

"I just hope to God they are."

"And I want to do it quiet and quick, Masao, because the tours keep coming. A bus moves into this square every three minutes and another one moves out. Everything is timed, controlled and staged. We could put five thousand people through the tour on a busy day, so just think of how that could be loused up. I get paid to keep things from getting loused up. All right, we'll work it out. Let's go into makeup now."

The room was for extras, for bit players, for second leads and any others who didn't have their own dressing rooms or their own makeup people. It was crowded, noisy, and dominated by a tall, hawk-faced, efficient woman with dark eyes and gray hair. This was Jesse Klein, and when she spotted Jefferson, her dour hatchet face broke into a grin and she yelled, "Hey, cowboy! We got a part for you in this one."

"Not me, bubby. You don't make no actor out of me."

"Why don't you stop with that bubby-business, you big ape? How do you think it sounds to people, the way you go around, bubby this and bubby that? Anyway, we're busy here. You don't want to act, you want to tear down the profession—beat it."

He took her arm, introduced Masuto softly, and asked her to step outside with them.

"That sounds like a dirty invitation."

"Come on, come on—stop with the wisecracks already, bubby."

"You know," she said, going out with them, "you got 1930 slang, old Franko. The kids don't say wisecracks anymore. There are no more wiseacres. That has gone the way of 23 skiddoo. Today you break them up or you're putting them on or you're bleeding on them or you're talking cockamamie or something. What do you want, anyway?"

"You know Phoebe Greenberg, bubby?"

"Sure I know her, poor kid. She inherited nothing but

lousy. Then she married poor Al, and the whole world said she had it made. Everyone—Phoebe, you got it made. You got the world by the short hairs. And everybody tells Al he married an angel. Are you a religious man, John Wayne?''

"I'll tell you what," Jefferson said. "You stop calling me John Wayne, I stop calling you bubby. Is that a deal?''

"It's a deal.''

"So I'm not religious, bubby.''

"All right—you religious?'' she asked Masuto.

"It's a foreign religion, so go right ahead.''

"Then I'll tell you about God. You want to know what God does for kicks? He's got these angels roaming the world, trying to find someone's happy or got it made. Then one of 'em yells up to God, 'Hey God, here's Phoebe down here. She's got it made!' Then? You know what then? Then—wham!''

"Sounds reasonable," Jefferson said. "The point is this. Phoebe is coming in in maybe ten, fifteen minutes, and she wants to be made up. She'll tell you how she wants to be made up. You make her up. You ask no questions. You make her up.''

"Just like that?''

"Just like that. She wants a costume, get it for her. Who's on wardrobe?''

"Bessie Kenning.''

Jefferson took a pad from his pocket and scribbled a few words. "Give that to Bessie," he told Jesse Klein, handing her the slip of paper.

"You don't want to tell me any more?''

"I don't want you to ask any more, bubby," he said. "I'll meet you at the cafeteria at one o'clock and I'll buy you lunch and I'll buy you an ice cream soda for desert, and we'll set the whole place talking about me. Then, if you behave, I may tell you what kind of tricks we're up to.''

"You're all heart," she said.

He walked down toward Stage 6 with Masuto. "Wait in the alley at the back," he said. "I'll have the three boys with you in ten minutes."

"Time's running out," Masuto said.

"Don't worry. They'll be there."

CHAPTER TEN

Captain Sharkman

Masuto was nervous. Time crowded him and caught up with him, and the whole machine was running too rapidly. He was a man who liked to think, who mistrusted quick conclusions, and now there was no time to think. He spent ten minutes waiting in the back alley, increasingly irritated as the minutes ticked by; and then when the three studio policemen appeared in uniform, his annoyance reached the bursting point.

"Why aren't you in plainclothes?" he demanded.

"Because nobody told us to get into plainclothes," one of them explained. "If you want us to, we'll go back and change."

Masuto's watch said ten forty. "No, it's too late. We'll make out." Masuto caught himself and calmed himself. In any case, it was not their fault. They simply did as they were told. Suddenly, he was almost physically sick with a wave of mistrust of Frank Jefferson. But then he overcame that. It was insane and pointless—and unless he controlled his thoughts and rode hard on his suspicions the entire fabric he was weaving would collapse. The point was not to mistrust Frank Jefferson, but to recognize an area of stupidity—which was always obvious in another person. It was his own errors, his own misjudgements and stupidities that might destroy him and Phoebe, not another's.

He explained the situation in as few words as possible.

"I want the killer," he said, "but above all, I want Mrs. Greenberg unharmed."

"Don't worry about that, Sergeant."

"Don't worry," Masuto said bitterly. "How the hell can I not worry when I am told that no guns are to be fired?"

"Unless we have to."

"What determines that?"

"Circumstances."

"I am armed," said Masuto. "If the killer has a gun, I'll use mine—that is, if the killer's gun threatens Mrs. Greenberg or myself. If the killer shows no gun, I won't use mine. Is that agreed?"

They nodded slowly.

"All right. I am going into the stage now. Remember—if possible I will come out of there into the street at nine minutes after eleven. I don't think so, but conceivably I could have a gun in my hand. Just take a long, hard look before you make any decision. That's nineteen minutes from now—right?"

"Right."

"Then take your posts and stay on them."

Then Masuto walked out of the back alley, turned right at the side alley, through the hard shadow into the burning white sunlight of the studio street. The candidates for murder were prompt, but perhaps that was to be expected. Trude Burke's MG was parked in front of the stage, and a grip was climbing in to return it to the parking lot. Sidney and Trude were standing at the door to Stage 6, and Sidney said cheerfully, "We're waiting, Sarge. I don't go in there without an escort."

At the same moment, a huge black Northeastern company limousine drew up to the soundstage, and the uniformed chauffeur opened the door for the five people inside: Murphy Anderson, Stacy Anderson, Jack Cotter, Arlene Cotter, and Lenore Tulley.

"We thought we'd come together," Anderson explained

to Masuto. "We wanted to bring Phoebe, but she had already left when I called her home."

"There was a message from her at the gate," Masuto told them. "There was some mix-up at the cemetery. Evidently, they had some sort of title problem about the grave site. She had to buy seven square feet of additional land, and there was nothing to it but they must have a certified check. She went to the bank first, then to the cemetery, and then she'll be here. It doesn't matter."

"We'll hold it up, then?" Cotter asked. They were all tense and nervous.

"No—no, we don't need Mrs. Greenberg."

"How do you know?" Cotter demanded.

"For Christ's sake, Jack—don't be a damn fool!" Stacy said.

Sidney and Trude Burke stepped over to join them, and Murphy Anderson said, "Hello, Sidney."

"I'm putting that in the record," Sidney said. "A leper needs hellos. He files them away. Take it from me, Murph—don't be Mr. Goodguy. No percentage."

"I don't like that," Cotter said. "You're too damn quick with that tongue of yours, Sidney, and one day you're going to choke on it."

"For crying out loud—" Anderson began. Cotter snapped at him, "Who the hell is Masuto here to act as any kind of judge and jury? It's no worse to think of Phoebe as the killer than it is to think of Trude as the killer—"

"Oh, drop dead," Trude told him. "I never knew a cowboy player who wasn't an idiot—so why don't you stop trying to be a bigger schmuck than God made you! Let's get inside and get this lousy horror over with."

"I'm for that," Lenore Tulley said.

Masuto opened the door to the soundstage, and Sidney went through and opened the inside sounddoor. One by one, they entered—Masuto last. It was exactly one minute after eleven o'clock.

Inside the door, they stood in a tight group, allowing

their eyes to become used to the dim light. Directly in front of them, a pile of cable lay like a tangle of enormous snakes in a jungle of arc lights and reflectors. There was a standing set of a modern kitchen, tiny and surrealist in the great enclosed space, and in the background one side of an ocean liner. Otherwise, only two high, half-drawn cycs and the shadowy spaces of roof, catwalks and far walls. Still, it was a dark forest—full of lairs and windfalls.

"Mrs. Greenberg left word that she would be here no later than eleven five, and it's almost that now," Masuto said.

"If Phoebe's pegged for the killer," Stacy said, "then I am getting out of here right now."

"No one said she is pegged for the killer," her husband reminded her.

"I hate this stage. Let's get out of here."

"I just realized," Trude said.

"What?"

"He got his first one here. This is where Freddie Saxton was killed. Of course."

"Which is why we're here, bright eyes," Sidney said. "And it's no he. We got a dirty-minded broad doing all this scragging."

They were drifting apart now, just as Masuto had predicted, gathering courage as they realized that the soundstage was only a soundstage—no more, no less.

"Clean-minded Sidney," Trude said. "That's why I married you, my turtle dove, because you're so clean-minded and sincere."

"You married me for my money."

"Big discovery."

Masuto said loudly, "Look, everyone—stay together and stay inside. For your own protection, stay together—and under no circumstances is anyone to leave the soundstage without permission from me—not until the witness arrives."

"Where is Phoebe?" Cotter demanded petulantly. He was over by one of the great cycs now, and he called out to Anderson, "Murph, this is ripped—did you know? They'll bill us for a new cyc—they come to about seven hundred dollars."

"The hell with it!" Anderson said. "Stop worrying about the goddamn cyc."

"Mr. Anderson," Masuto said, "I'm stepping to the door to see if Mrs. Greenberg arrived. I'll be back in a moment."

"Sure." Then Anderson called to Cotter, "Anyway, I think that cyc was torn before. Forget it."

Masuto stepped through the soundstage door into the street, blinking in the hot sunlight. The soundstage had been dim, cool and silent. Out here, a steam calliope was blaring circus music from the other side of the square. Buses with their brightly stripped awnings of yellow and black were rolling in and out of the square, and under the guidance of young men and women in costume, crowds of tourists were being ushered through the carpentry shop and the plaster shop and the mocked-up Soundstage 11 to see all the wonders of how movies were made. There were kids eating ice cream cones and popcorn and frankfurters, boys and girls holding hands, cowboys, Indians and gay Western ladies of the movie saloons. And through it all moved the grotesque lumbering figures who were America's cartoon heroes—Captain Devildom, with five wiggling tentacles and a ray gun; Major Meridean, dressed like a gladiator but with a rocket belt that could zip him anywhere in the world to right wrongs and defeat master criminals; Space Ace Ambrose in his gleaming space suit of red, white, and blue anodized aluminum, and other symbols of character and courage.

The calliope was screaming out a Sousa march as Masuto crossed the street, turning to face the soundstage. At the far end of the stage, the uniformed studio guard stepped out of the alley and lounged a few steps down the street,

so that he could watch the door without appearing too
obvious.

At the same moment, out of the corner of his eyes,
Masuto saw Phoebe leave Stage 9 and start toward him. At
least, he was certain that the stout, dark-haired woman—
hair graying and wearing a cheap blue cotton dress that fell
four inches below her knees—was Phoebe Greenberg. It
had to be. Yet he wouldn't have believed that any makeup
could be so perfect.

Then she met his eyes and they exchanged glances and
he made a slight circle of approval with his middle finger
and his thumb and she dropped one lid, and he knew that it
was Phoebe. But in that time, for one part of a moment,
for one part of a second, he made the error of negligence
and sheer stupidity that he was destined to make. For one
instant, he took his eyes off the soundstage door. When he
glanced at it again, Captain Sharkman stood in the street in
front of the stage.

Even in that instant, Masuto could not help thinking
what a remarkable and impressive costume it was. It was
mad, but then the world was mad and this was a dream
factory out of which rolled, day in and day out, the
fantasies, romances and nightmares of an entire nation.
This was why a thousand generations had lived and died
and fought and toiled—so that an apparation called Captain Sharkman could strut slowly toward him on the sun-
soaked studio street. Captain Sharkman was six and a half
feet tall. From the waist down, each leg was the separate
body of a shark, an astonishing imitation of the pasty
white skin of the fish itself. The torso was white and pale
gray, and the arms were two ugly appendages that ended
in sharkfins, and the head was a shark's head, ugly,
expressionless, uptilted with the undercut jaw open. Through
that opening, Captain Sharkman had vision, but the mask
was cleverly constructed and no eyeholes were apparent.
And on either side of Captain Sharkman's head, a pair of

moist red gills moved in slow rhythm. Two red, white and blue striped epaulets gave him his rank.

During the next few seconds, things happened very quickly. Masuto saw the studio guard staring at Captain Sharkman but making no move to stop him. "Look for a murderer," he had been told. But no one told him to look for Captain Sharkman. If a decision was difficult for Masuto to make, it was impossible for the guard. If the guard followed Captain Sharkman, the door would be left unguarded.

And what do I do? Masuto asked himself.

But there was nothing to do. Captain Sharkman shuffled up the street toward him. Phoebe walked across the square toward him. Masuto stood and waited, and a tour bus slowly moved across the top of the street toward the high mesquite hills on the back lot. The plan, prepared so carefully, had come to pieces.

Masuto made his decision. He let go of his plan and he let go of Phoebe. It was wrong, and he wanted her out of there, and as the bus crossed in front of her, he yelled, "Get on that bus!"

She had a mind and she had good reactions. Masuto watched with pleasure how specifically and quickly she reacted to his command, stepping onto the bus as if she had been waiting for it, standing on the running board and hanging onto one of the steel uprights that supported the awning. The passengers giggled with pleasure at her makeup and costume, and the driver-guide spoke into his microphone, "One of our Western ladies of small repute, friends, right out of a border saloon, yes, sir—one of the many surprises—"

Captain Sharkman broke into an entirely unexpected and most unlikely sprint, swinging onto the running board on the opposite side of the bus, hooking an arm-fin around the steel support. Masuto raced after him, caught the upright at the very end of the bus and hung on there as the bus rolled out of the square and onto the beginning of the mountain road, and still Masuto did not know for certain whether the murderer was on the bus here with him or back on Soundstage 6, chatting with the others and laughing quietly at Masuto's stupidity. Well, that's the way it was; you were brilliant and intuitive and you built a plan step by step and removed every wrinkle and considered that finally it was foolproof, and then the unexpected.

"An unexpected pleasure," the driver said into the microphone that curved toward him from under his rear-view mirror. "Here we have Captain Sharkman himself. Well, that's something to talk about, isn't it? We are taking the hairpin climb up there to the Peak of Despondency, and you can see the Norman tower up there built for the great remake of 'The Conqueror'—and we have two studio guests, this little lady from the old West and Captain Sharkman. In case any of you have not had the pleasure of watching Captain Sharkman perform his great deeds on TV, I can tell you that he is one of the great cartoon stars of Grapheonics, and he does his part in righting wrong, preventing crime, and defending the American way of life. In his college days, Captain Sharkman was all-American—at the Naval Academy. Three years after his graduation he was in command of an atomic submarine, the ill-fated Finray that exploded off the coast of Africa in 1961. But by some miracle of electronics, instead of dying in that atomic blast, Captain Sharkman and his crew were transformed in a strange evolutionary process provoked by the atomic blast. They became sharkmen, and so were able to continue their lives and adventures in defense of the free world and the American way—"

As the spiel droned on, the driver was manipulating the hairpin turns of the studio road, climbing higher and higher, until Masuto could see below him the studio laid out, sound stages like small blocks, and beyond the studio the whole hazy vista of the San Fernando Valley.

"You will all recollect," the driver continued, "that

unfortunate accident in which an atomic bomb was lost off the coast of Spain. Well, we like to think that Captain Sharkman and his crew of fearless underwater heroes were instrumental in recovering it, and in their dangerous underwater existence, this is only one of their many, many tasks. At the top of the climb, at the Peak of Despondency, there is a souvenir and refreshment counter where you can purchase a small replica of Captain Sharkman, either entirely assembled or in plastic pieces, one dollar—''

They had slowed almost to a stop to take one of the hairpin turns and Masuto shouted, "Phoebe, drop off!''

Again, she obeyed. She dropped off the bus onto the edge of the road. Masuto dropped off. It hung in the balance, and then as the bus rounded the curve, Masuto saw that Captain Sharkman had also dropped off.

It had worked. Masuto faced the murderer. Phoebe ran a few steps, and then she was next to Masuto. "Behind me and down the road," he snapped at her. He had drawn his pistol, and as Captain Sharkman came toward them, Masuto pointed the gun and said, "Don't make me kill you.''

A hundred yards up the road and fifty feet above them, the bus had stopped, the passengers staring at what was happening below. The driver yelled, "What goes on there, old buddy?''

The passengers giggled self-consciously.

Phoebe paused a few yards behind Masuto, and now Captain Sharkman leaped toward Masuto.

Masuto fired twice at Captain Sharkmen's legs. Either the costume deflected the bullets or Masuto missed, and then Captain Sharkman was upon him, and a blow of the big armfin knocked the gun out of Masuto's hand. As he attempted to lunge past Masuto, the detective caught him with a backhand karate chop, knocking him off balance. Sharkman slipped, stumbled and then caught himself. The two of them dropped into karate position now, and Masuto realized that his right hand was bleeding from the blow with the fin. The fin was hard as steel and rough to

simulate real sharkskin. It would only take a single karate
chop with that rocklike fin to stop Masuto, to break a neck
or an arm or a shoulder—and Captain Sharkman was
determined to have the blow, to bring it in, to finish
Masuto and get the girl. He was senseless now, mindless,
and he rushed Masuto and screamed as he made his chop.

It missed. The audience in the bus shouted with excitement and howled with laughter.

Masuto's own cry came with the blow he launched. It
was the explosive karate sound, and his hand chopped into
Sharkman's neck and hit plastic and foam rubber. He hit
again as Sharkman lumbered for his own position. Masuto
was quicker, like a mongoose with a cobra, but Sharkman
was almost invulnerable in his cocoon of plastic and foam
rubber. Again and again, Sharkman swung his lethal fin,
and again and again Masuto avoided it—only once not
entirely, and it opened his left sleeve and took the surface
skin off his left arm, shoulder to elbow.

It was then that Phoebe was able to dart in and pick up
Masuto's gun, and as the crowd in the bus hooted and
yelled and screamed, "Fake! Watch it, Sharkman—they
got a gun!"

Phoebe cried to him, "Masao—here's your gun!"

Masuto got the gun, but Phoebe was not quick enough
and a glancing blow from the fin sent her sprawling on the
road. Masuto fired point-blank at Captain Sharkman's head.
Sharkman wheeled around, and Masuto fired twice into the
open mouth—and Sharkman staggered back, back from
the edge of the road, fell and rolled down, down the slope,
breaking mesquite and cactus and finally coming to a stop
in the little drainage culvert that was the edge of the lower
turn of the road.

Masuto helped Phoebe to her feet. She rubbed her
shoulder.

"It's not broken, is it?"

"It feels like it's broken into twenty pieces. Oh—Masao,
it hurts like hell."

"See if you can move your arm."

She moved her arm tentatively. "It hurts, but I can move it." She pulled off the black wig. "I look rotten as a brunette," she said.

"It beats me," Masuto said softly. "It just beats me."

A bus climbing the hill had stopped, and the tourists were crowding around Mr. Sharkman, and the tourists from the bus above were arguing with the driver, who was trying to keep them from pouring down the road.

Helping Phoebe, Masuto went down the road, and when the bus driver began his protest, Masuto said tiredly, "Damn it, I'm a cop. So why don't you see if you can back down the road and get Frank Jefferson and tell him there's been trouble here and he should get to hell up here."

"You can't back down that road."

"Then run down it by foot, damn you!"

Meanwhile, two people in the crowd around Captain Sharkman were easing off his headpiece.

"What are you doing?" Masuto demanded.

"I'm a doctor," a small man with glasses said. "This man is hurt. I don't know what you did to him with that gun you have in your hand—"

"Then help him," Masuto said without feeling.

Phoebe, next to him, was shivering. She pressed up against him as they removed the headpiece.

"Oh, my God, it's Jack Cotter!" Phoebe said.

"Didn't you know?"

A bullet had gone through his neck, but there was no blood on his face. It was pasty white, puffy; he looked like a pudgy, harmless man with pale blue eyes. The doctor bent over him for a minute or so, and then turned to Masuto and said, "Well, he's dead."

Masuto shrugged.

"Well, who are you, mister?" the doctor demanded.

"I'm a cop," Masuto said, putting the gun away in his jacket pocket.

"And who is he?"

Phoebe began to cry, and Masuto put his arm around her.

"That arm of yours needs attention," the doctor said to Masuto. "That's a pretty bad scrape."

Still Masuto stared at Cotter, and then he said quietly to Phoebe, "Stop crying. There's no need to cry now."

"He was Al's friend."

"He was nobody's friend," Masuto said.

"There's a dead man there," the doctor said. "I'm asking you who he is?"

"He's Captain Sharkman," Masuto said, and then he pulled Phoebe out of the crowd and they began to walk down the road back to the studio.

The bus driver yelled after them, "Mister, if you're a cop, what am I supposed to do with this stiff?"

"Leave it alone," Masuto said.

But now Jefferson was on his way, his long black car with its spinning top light of bright red and its screaming siren careening up the mountain road and then pulling to a stop alongside of Phoebe and Masuto. There was a driver, Jefferson and two uniformed guards, and the two guards leaped out of the car and Jefferson put on his best John Wayne manner, looming over Masuto and demanding, "What the hell kind of bad business is this, Masao. I tell you no shooting and you gun a man down."

Masuto glanced at his left arm, the blood welling out of the long, ugly scrape, and said that he was sorry.

"Was it your man?"

"That's right."

"Was your guess right?"

"It was right," Masuto said.

"Well, I'll be damned. You just never know, do you?"

"You never know," Masuto agreed.

"That arm looks ugly, bubby," Jefferson said. "Get it tended to. You know where the studio clinic is."

"I know."

"I'd ride you down, but we got things up here. Can you walk?"

"I can walk."

"It's not bleeding very much. Just an ooze."

"I'll walk and I'll survive."

"We stopped the tour for the time being," Jefferson said. "I guess we'll lose maybe two hours. You know what that costs the studio."

"My heart is breaking," Masuto said.

"I can just see that. Look, when you get that arm fixed up, come around to my office. I want a statement from you. Also, I got to call in the LA cops."

"I'll come around," Masuto said.

They got back in the car and drove up the road to where the bus was parked and where the crowd of tourists could not pull themselves away from Jack Cotter's body. Masuto and Phoebe were alone on the road now. They stood there for a moment, and then Phoebe said, "That arm does look awful."

"It looks worse than it is. It's not really bleeding, and unless you're going to dress one of those bad scrapes, the best thing is to leave it alone."

"But doesn't it hurt terribly?"

"It hurts."

"You're a strange man," she said.

He shrugged and pointed down the road. "It's a long walk," he said.

They walked on in silence for a while, and then she said, "You knew right along that it was Jack Cotter?"

"Yes."

"I'm going to be sick," she announced suddenly.

"Try not to be."

"I can't try not to be. I can't control it."

He supported her by the side of the road as she heaved and cried out in pain.

"Easy, Phoebe—what is it?"

"My shoulder. It hurts so when I throw up. Oh, I am so miserable."

"Do you feel better now?"

"A little," she said. "I feel a little better."

They began to walk again, slowly, Phoebe hanging onto Masuto's right arm. Phoebe asked him, "When did you know it was Jack Cotter."

"The first night. In the viewing room at your house."

"No. How could you?"

"Because only he heard Samantha's voice. No one else. Every one took it for granted that it was a woman, but no one else heard the voice."

"Then whose voice did Lenore Tulley hear?"

"Jack Cotter's. Maybe he was a rotten actor, but how good do you have to be to talk in falsetto?"

She walked on for a while, and then she shook her head and said, "I don't understand, Masao. Why? Why did he kill Freddie Saxton? Why did he kill Mike Tulley? Why did he kill Al?"

"Why does a killer kill? He had a motive—he wanted Northeastern Films. He wanted to be it, the top man, the owner, the boss. But for that he only had to get rid of two men, Murphy Anderson and your husband. But that would point directly to him, wouldn't it? So he decided that Samantha would do it, and he killed Mike Tulley and Fred Saxton to establish the Samantha-revenge motive."

"But that's insane."

"He was insane."

"You mean he began this seven weeks ago, and that he then murdered Fred Saxton only to lay the basis for linking Samantha to the other killings?"

"That's right. As a matter of fact, I imagine he got the idea a year ago, when your assistant producer, Max Green, died of a heart attack."

"It doesn't seem possible."

"Murder never seems possible—and this kind of insane,

grotesque murder is even less than possible. Only, it happens.''

''And that poor woman, Peggy Groton, who died up on Mulholland Drive—did he kill her too?''

''Yes.''

''But why?''

''Do you remember the phone call from Samantha—the one received in the office?''

''In the office? Oh, yes—yes, Murph told me about it.''

''Well, Cotter could imitate a woman's voice to the extent of a few words through a locked door—but not a whole conversation over the telephone. That had to be a real woman, and any woman who became a part of his lunatic murder scheme was doomed. He couldn't allow Peggy Groton to live, not for an hour, not for a half hour. He had to kill her and kill her quickly.''

''Poor Al,'' she said. ''Poor Al. He never had an enemy. Can you imagine living in this place and not having an enemy? Do you know, Masao, if we walked down the street and a panhandler stopped him, he never said no. He was the industry touch. You were never in the industry, so you don't know what I mean, but no one ever asked Al and was turned down. And then that fool of a Jack Cotter, that strutting, ridiculous cowboy hero—there'll never be a day of my life when I won't think of him killing Al, and Al pleading for that medicine that held his life—''

''But we'll never know,'' Masuto said. ''It's always possible that he didn't kill your husband. Mr. Greenberg could have had a heart attack and Cotter could have taken advantage of it.''

''And we won't know, will we?''

''I'm afraid not.''

''You know, I have a feeling that if you let go of me, I'd be hysterical.''

''No, you'll be all right.''

''Will you come and talk to the others? Do you suppose they're still there—on Stage 6?''

"Why not? It's less than an hour since I left them."

"Will you talk to them?"

"No," Masuto said.

"Why not? Do you despise us so?"

"I don't despise you."

"What do you call it, Masao?"

"I don't despise you. I don't judge you."

"And isn't that a typical statement for those you despise?"

"No."

"It's so easy for you. You live behind that damned Oriental mask of yours—"

Masuto felt himself freezing, closing up.

"I'm sorry," she said. "Dear Masao—I am so terribly sorry. I don't know why I said that."

"You said it because you felt it."

"Oh, Christ—no. No. Don't talk to me like that, Masao."

"I don't know of any other way to talk to you, Mrs. Greenberg."

"Sure. There it is. You've got that great big goddamn Japanese mask spread all over your face, and lump me and all that I am because I can never get past it, and what am I anyway but a skinny, washed-out Anglo-Saxon blond bitch who was just hanging onto you and vomiting over the side of the road; and two days after my husband died, here I am trying to make a pass at you—so why don't you just spit in my face instead of going through this damned *Sayonara* politeness routine!"

He stopped and turned to face her. They were almost down at the square now, and he could see that it was filled with tourists from the stopped buses, and an ambulance was squeezing through to come up the road, and behind the ambulance there was a Los Angeles police car, and they would be up next to him in a minute or two and what does one say in a minute or two that can explain the whole world and the way it is?

"Phoebe," he cried, "Phoebe, what in hell are you doing to me? I'm a Japanese, and the hell with this Nisei business! I am a cop. I take home one hundred and forty-two dollars each week, and they give me a car. I am married. I have three kids. In all her life my wife never set foot in a home like yours, but she has a sister who works in one as a maid. My wife never used a foul word or ever lifted her voice in anger against me or one of my kids. I am not a Jew or a Christian or a Mormon or anything else that would have any meaning for you, and I love you but I will get over it. So help me God, I will get over it. And that's it. The end of it. The finish of it. No more.''

Then the ambulance reached them, and she knew what he said was true and would hold.

At the studio clinic, while Masuto's arm was being dressed and while his jacket was being mended by one of the wardrobe tailors, a stream of people passed by to check his credentials and to hear his side of the story. Studio executives, Los Angeles cops, the district attorney, sheriff's deputies.

Finally his own Chief listened to what he had to say and then told him, ''Good enough, Masao. You can have the rest of the day off.''

''The redheaded one, Trude Burke, you know what she would say to that?''

''What would she say, Masao?''

''You're all heart. That's what she would say.''

''Don't rate me, Masao. It's the taxpayers' money.''

''Sure, it's the taxpayers' money.''

''Anyone else would drag you down to the office for a full statement. I'm willing to wait a couple of days.''

''Like I said, you're all heart.''

''Yeah. Can you drive or do you want a chauffeur?''

''I can drive.''

The arm hurt a bit, but it did not interfere with his driving, but at home, when his wife, Kati, put her hand on his arm, he winced with pain—and then he had to tell her most of what had happened. As she listened, her eyes filled with tears at the thought of the danger he had faced.

She served him a very simple lunch of tea-rice and green tea, and then he went out to the garden to fuss with his roses. She brought out her basket of mending and she sat quietly by the back door of the house, doing her sewing while he pruned branches, cut roses, loosened soil and sprayed just a bit here and there. There was still an hour before the children returned from school, and an hour like this, with Masao in the garden and herself sitting by quietly with her work, was almost better than anything else in the world.

SCENE OF THE CRIME

ROBERT BARNARD

Keen on "whodunits" in the classic British style? You'll find these, dear reader, bloody good —and murderously funny.